COME TO ME

SIERRA CARTWRIGHT

HAWKEYE

COME TO ME

DEDICATION

For Rene Webb who challenged me to show longer Happily Ever Afters. This one's for you!

For BAB and the midnight oil—as always.

Riane, I'm so glad I get to work with you!

CHAPTER ONE

HAWKEYE

S *hit.*

    Nate Davidson opened his eyes and tried to shake away the stars that had exploded in his head and stolen his vision. It took several tries before the image of strong, tall, dark, and dangerous Wolf Stone blinked into focus. And when it did, Nate was certain he'd never seen anything better.

It'd been a long time. Too damn long.

"You're lucky I didn't tear your fool head off."

Nate flexed his jaw to make sure it still worked. "Feels to me like you did."

"What the fuck are you doing here?" Stone's voice was deep and ragged, cut glass on velvet.

"You're not glad to see me? I thought you'd start looking for a fattened calf." Nate knew what real danger was. It had nothing to do with his battered body or the nasty storm snarling its way over the Rocky Mountains. Danger was Wolf Stone. And Nate was in the bigger, stronger man's sights.

Nate struggled to get his elbows behind him. Damn

mountains were made of rock, not the best pillow under any circumstances. Downright painful when you'd had your clock cleaned by a tank of a man. "Mind if I sit up?"

"Stay where you are."

Lying on the ground, looking well over six feet up into Stone's cold blue eyes left Nate at a disadvantage—or, rather, at a greater disadvantage than he usually was around Stone. "Hospitable as always, aren't you, boss?"

"All trespassers get the same treatment."

No matter how hard either of them tried to pretend otherwise, they both knew Nate was no ordinary trespasser.

And Stone was no ordinary property owner.

He'd commanded several missions that Nate had been assigned to. Every person selected had to meet rigorous physical standards. By any measure, Nate was a good-size man, an inch over six feet, two hundred seven pounds of lean muscle.

Still, Stone had him by two inches and at least twenty pounds. Even now, recouping from injuries, Stone had effortlessly brought Nate down. Well, that was an understatement. Stone had tossed Nate like an old magazine.

"Still waiting for an answer to my question, Davidson."

Sometimes, only the truth would do. "When you refused protection, Hawkeye sent me."

"You're here," Stone demanded incredulously, "to protect *me*?" He raised a dark eyebrow in a way that made grown men cower. Nate had seen it happen, and he refused to admit to himself that it made him cower as well.

"Who'd have imagined?" *Ludicrous.*

Stone sheathed his knife. The weapon was overkill. He only needed his hands in order to tear a strip out of someone's hide.

"Tell Hawkeye I said thanks, but no thanks. You can find your own way off the ranch." Stone turned.

If he hadn't been looking for it, Nate might not have noticed Stone's slight limp. *Stubborn man.* The threat against his life was real and imminent. He was the only eyewitness to the hit that had taken out Elliott and Lisa Mulgrew. Word on the street was that some lucky bastard would get a cool million dollars if Stone didn't make it to court to testify against Michael Huffman, the murderer.

While Stone was holed up in his fortress, he was safe enough. But once he left Cold Creek Ranch, he'd need the backup.

"So," Nate called out when Stone got about ten paces away, "you're not interested in knowing how I breached the perimeter?"

"You got exactly nowhere before your ass was mine." He continued on without looking back.

"Storm's brewing, man!"

"You'll get wet."

Well, hell. Nate collapsed back onto the unforgiving ground. That'd gone well.

Stone disappeared over a ridge, vanishing into thick Ponderosa pines.

In a nearby tree, a hairy woodpecker—nasty little bastard —beat out a staccato that matched the throbbing headache in Nate's temples.

Under any circumstances, he deferred to Stone. The man exuded a palpable loyalty-inspiring authority. Even now, when Stone didn't want assistance, didn't want to be protected, Nate had no intention of leaving. Stone was as determined as the mountains were rugged. Then again, so was Nate.

Hawkeye hadn't recruited Nate for this job. He, plus the helicopter pilot and copilot, had volunteered. It had taken days of planning, and he refused to admit failure.

Half a dozen raindrops pelted his cheeks.

Even in the past few minutes, the storm had gathered clouds and whipped them together with wind to descend the eastern slope of the Continental Divide.

Could this get any worse?

Lightning slashed through the swollen gray sky, igniting a path of cloud-to-cloud strikes.

Yeah. It had gotten worse.

WOLF STONE, NO MATTER HOW DROP-DEAD GORGEOUS HE WAS, was out of his freaking mind. And an asshole to boot. "You left Nate out there?" Kayla Fagan demanded. "Have you seen the weather?"

"He's not made of sugar."

"Meaning he won't melt?"

"Exactly."

"If this is how you treat your fellow operatives, what do you do to your enemies?"

He shrugged. "None of them left alive to tell." He smiled, and it did nothing to soften his features. The quick curve was more wicked than anything, making his eyes darken, reminding her of those few moments of twilight before the sky devoured the sun.

He strode from the kitchen, and she followed. "Mr. Stone—"

"Wolf, or just Stone." He didn't slow down. "And I'm not worried about how I'll sleep tonight." He crouched in front of the hearth, tossing kindling into the empty fireplace grate.

When she first heard he was holing up in a log house on a ranch, she'd pictured a remote, barely inhabitable two-room cabin.

She couldn't have been more wrong.

Wolf Stone enjoyed luxury, and his home was the intersection of comfort and high-tech. This room, more than any other, gave a nod to his heritage. A rug, painstakingly woven by his grandmother, hung from one of the walls. Another rug, not crafted by his family, dominated the area near the fireplace.

In other rooms, he flicked a switch to ignite the gas fireplaces, but in this one, he obviously preferred to build it himself.

Even though she was stunned by his bad behavior, she couldn't help her fascination as she watched him. His shoulders were impossibly broad. Long black hair, as wild as he was, was cinched back with a thin strip of leather. And Lord, he had the hottest ass she'd ever seen, and a cock with plenty of potential.

Not that she'd actually seen it full-length.

But at night, when he thought she was asleep, he walked around the house in the buff.

Last night, his dick had been partially erect, and the darkened view had inspired her dreams and nearly made her forget her job.

Lucky for her, at least part of the time, she was required to have her hands on him. She just hadn't quite figured out how to professionally get him to take off all his clothes to touch his naked body.

Thunder cracked, and she worried about Nate. "I think you should at least invite him in until the storm passes." Even though it was summer, weather could be extreme at this elevation.

"You going to nag me?"

"Convince you to change your mind, using my excellent powers of verbal persuasion."

"Save your breath. Hawkeye doesn't need to squander its resources on me."

Hawkeye Security. The company they all worked for was

named after the man who'd founded it, a man she, and most others, had never met. Wolf, she'd heard, was one of his closest advisors.

With their highly trained men and women, Hawkeye provided world-renowned protection. They recruited former Special Forces operators, ex-cops, bodyguards, lots of IT people, and other brainiacs, including some who worked remotely out of small, private offices. The higher the stakes, the likelier it was that Hawkeye would be the firm of choice.

Her teammates were the best in the world. She was proud to be one of them. "Hawkeye brought me in as well," she reminded him. "Maybe he would go to these extraordinary lengths for any one of us, but maybe he wouldn't. All I can say is he obviously considers you important."

Stone struck a match, filling the room with the sharpness of sulfur. "My mind is made up."

"But—"

"I told Hawkeye not to send anyone. I meant it."

"You can have a heart, just until the weather clears. Then you can go back to your regularly scheduled..." She stopped short of saying assholeishness. "Grumpiness."

His mouth was set, brooking no argument. "Let it be."

Huge splatters of rain hit the floor-to-ceiling windowpanes.

Wolf might be able to sleep at night if he left his comrade out there, but she would toss and turn with worry.

Decision made, Kayla crossed to the hallway closet, pulled open the gigantic golden oak doors, and took out a raincoat. She also grabbed her gun and checked it before tucking it into her waistband. She snatched up a pair of compact binoculars and a compass and was shoving her arms in the sleeves of the yellow slicker as she walked through the great room on the way to the back door.

"What do you think you're doing?"

"Exactly what you said. I'm saving my breath." Kayla spared him a glance. "I decided not to argue with you."

"Stop right there."

He spoke softly, but his voice snapped with whiplash force. Despite herself, she froze. She'd faced untold danger, but this man, unarmed, unnerved her. A funny little knot formed in the pit of her stomach.

Kindling crackled as fire gnawed its edges.

"Turn around." His voice was terrifying in its quietness. "Look at me, Fagan."

Struggling not to show the way she was trembling, she turned.

He stood. "I will be very clear, Ms. Fagan. You are here at my pleasure." He took a single step toward her. "I will not be disobeyed."

His statement was loaded with threat.

Wildly she thought of the room in the basement, the one with crops and paddles hanging from the walls. The one she'd been forbidden to enter, and the door she'd opened the first time he'd left the house.

She locked her knees so she didn't waver. "I've never been much for obedience."

"Nathaniel Davidson is far from helpless."

"He's a fellow member of Hawkeye. I'm not allowed to leave him out there. And I won't." She met his gaze and ignored the fury blazing there. "Really, Mr. Stone, I don't care if it gets me fired." *Or worse.* She pivoted and walked away.

The wind whipped at the door, nearly snatching it from her hand.

She turned up the collar of her ineffective raincoat. There was never anything friendly about a Rocky Mountain storm.

She'd grown up in Tucson where torrential rains were common during the monsoon season. They cooled the

weather to bearable seventy-degree temperatures, but this—
it was freaking like winter.

Fortunately, she didn't have far to trudge. From her
conversations with headquarters, she had a pretty good idea
of where the insertion was supposed to happen. And in less
than fifteen minutes, the ground beneath her sizzling with
electrical ferociousness, she saw a streak of orange.

She grinned.

Members of her team were smart. Nate had donned a
reflective safety vest. That would, at least, stop friendly fire.

"Davidson!" When she got no response, she called out a
second time.

He started toward her. "Come to rescue me, have you?" he
shouted above the roar of the wind. "Bet Stone told you to
come."

"He sends his regards and invites you to sit next to the
fire while he pours you a cognac."

Nate laughed. "How much trouble are you in for coming
after me?"

"He didn't threaten to flay the skin from my hide."

"Doesn't mean he won't."

"Thanks. That's a comforting thought."

"He doesn't know?"

"Who I am? No." She shook her head. "He thinks
Hawkeye sent him a physical therapist."

Nate grinned. "Do you know enough about that to do no
harm, doc?"

"Uh… I watched a special on the internet."

Thunder crashed.

"I ought to write both of you up."

Wolf. Her breath threatened to choke her. How much had
he overheard? It shouldn't have surprised her that he'd
followed, that he'd effortlessly covered the same ground she
had in far less time. The man was in shape, and he kept

himself sharp, the same way he had when he led American troops in the Middle East.

Over the lash of the summer storm, his voice laden with command, he said, "Both of you, back to the house."

The wind snatched a few strands of hair and whipped them against cheekbones that could have been sculptured from granite. His jaw was set in an uncompromising line. Out here, in the unforgiving elements, he appeared even more formidable than he had in the house.

Nate glanced at her. "Maybe I will get a cognac after all."

"No fucking chance," Stone fired back.

Cheerfully, as if he couldn't have been happier, Nate whistled and gamely started down the mountainside. No one should be happy about this kind of reception.

"Move it, Fagan," Stone instructed, leaning forward so he could issue his command directly into her ear.

"Yes, sir."

"Did you say something?"

She blinked innocently.

His arched brow told her he hadn't bought it.

Steps short but sure, she followed Nate, leaving Stone to bring up the rear.

Minutes later, the mean-looking sky unleashed a torrent. Earth became mud. Rocks became as slick as ice.

She lost her balance, and Stone was there, wrapping an arm around her waist, pulling her up and back, flush against the solidness of his body.

The sensation zinging through her was from him, not the streak of lightning. "I'm good. Fine."

He held her for a couple of seconds, his warm breath fanning across her ear. What would happen if she leaned back for just a bit longer and allowed herself to be protected in his strong arms? To feel his cock against her? To surrender to the fantasies that kept her awake at night and her pussy damp, even now?

And what fantasies they were.

Last night's sight of his semierect dick had driven her mad.

After he returned to his own room, she'd thought of the crops and paddles in his downstairs room. She'd pictured him using them on her while she gasped and strained, and ultimately surrendered to the inevitable. Turned on and needy, she'd pulled up her sleep shirt and parted her labia to find her clit already hardened.

She'd come with a quiet little mew and wanted nothing more than to scream the house down as his cock pounded her.

What was wrong with her? She couldn't afford thoughts like this with any man, particularly one she was sent to protect. Because of the risk inherent in working for Hawkeye Security, many employees were fueled by adrenaline, and affairs were common. But everyone knew the rules. No commitments. No emotions were allowed to get in the way of the job. But the way he held her was an invitation she wanted to accept. "You can let me go. It's you who needs to be careful. Otherwise we'll be spending the next week undoing the damage."

"So speaks my *physical therapist*."

Did he know who she was?

Before she had a chance to reply, he added, "I want you out of the storm."

He released her, and the chill crept under her jacket. This time, being more careful, she followed Nate's path.

The trip up had taken maybe about fifteen minutes. Down took half an hour. And by the time they reached the home's patio with its outdoor kitchen and oversize hot tub, the sky was spitting out pieces of ice in the form of hail.

Very polite country, this.

Minding her manners, she took off her shoes and left them on a rubber mat, then hung the slicker on a peg.

Kayla told herself two lies. First, that she wasn't stalling. Second, that her fingers were shaking because of the cold weather.

Stone unlocked the back door and indicated she should precede both men into the kitchen.

Nate followed her, and then Stone relocked the door behind them.

"You." Stone pointed a finger at Nate. "What the hell were you thinking?"

Nate took a step back for self-preservation.

Both men dripped water and tracked mud. Neither seemed to care. And neither seemed to notice she was even there.

"Hawkeye didn't assign you," Stone surmised.

"No," Nate said.

"Which means you volunteered." The storm hadn't remained outside. It had gathered force around Wolf and its heat threatened to consume them all.

Nate's retreat was brought up short when he backed into the countertop. "So? What of it?"

"You knew I wouldn't invite you here."

Nate shrugged. "You don't want anyone. Because you're a fool."

"A *fool*?"

"For always thinking you can do it alone. And you damn well know it."

The men were a study in contrast. Fair to dark. Alpha to beta.

"Fuck your ego, Stone. There's no place I'd rather be." Nate's tone was flat, as if that explained everything.

Kayla sucked in a breath when Wolf devoured the

distance to pin Nate against the counter. Nowhere to run. Nowhere to hide.

"Wolf," she said, licking her lower lip.

"You." He shot Kayla a frightening glance. "I will deal with you directly."

Her stomach plummeted to her toes. She was watching two magnificent warriors spar, and if she wasn't careful, she'd be collateral damage.

Wolf returned his attention to Nate, capturing the man's head between his palms and holding him prisoner.

What the hell...?

Wolf kissed Nate. Thoroughly. Punishingly. Brutally.

Her breath hissed out in stunned surprise.

Nate Davidson and Wolf Stone were *gay?*

Her world turned upside down and inside out. How could two virile, handsome, masculine men—men that she wanted to have sex with—possibly be gay?

.

CHAPTER TWO

HAWKEYE

"Nice to see you, too," Nate said when Stone ended the kiss. The man had all but shoved his tongue down his throat. He'd barely had time to breathe, and he tasted the potency of Irish whiskey on Stone's tongue.

It had taken mere seconds for Nate's cock to become hard and insistent. Carnal desire curled in his stomach. He wanted this man's domination, craved it. All the anger, the frustration, the neediness that had built over the past year crashed into him.

Stone's dick was as hard as his own. He might tell Nate his presence wasn't wanted at the ranch, but Stone's body said something else entirely.

If his onetime lover said the word, Nate would drop his pants and be bent over the end of the bed so fast ...

Then, aware of Kayla's wide, unblinking eyes, he said to Stone, "I think we've shocked Kayla. But I'm betting it won't be the last time."

"I'm...errr..." Kayla cleared her throat. "Surprised. I had no idea."

"That?"

"You're both gay."

"I'm bi," Nate said. "As for Stone, as long as he's in charge, he's happy."

"I can wait in the other room," she said. "Or brew coffee. Coffee's good."

"Coffee's good," Stone agreed. "Since everyone is so worried about Davidson, we should probably get him warmed up."

"Hypothermia is a possibility." As always, Nate's response was good-natured. "Or I could have been incinerated by lightning. Did you know Colorado ranks third, nationally, in lightning fatalities? Leading state in the West."

"You have no idea what a relief it is to know that I have two weather reporters in my house."

"Happy to help," Nate said.

"Since you're here, you might as well change into dry clothes."

"You mean I finally have the chance to get in your pants?"

"Forget coffee," Kayla said. "I'm going to open a bottle of wine."

Nate grinned. "Pour me a glass?" Then to his reluctant host, he asked, "Mind if I shower?"

"You've already invited yourself in."

The words were grudging and had more than a little bite of sarcasm. But Nate had gotten what he wanted. He was here. Stone had kissed him so hard that the burn of whiskey now lingered on Nate's tongue.

Grinning, he grabbed an apple from the fruit bowl and then headed down the hallway, past the guest bathroom and toward the master suite. Nate was already in trouble. Might as well see how far he could actually push it.

Stone's bedroom was much like the man himself. Rigid.

Everything where it belonged. Methodical. The dresser had nothing on its top. From past experience, Nate knew he'd find a loaded pistol, along with car keys and a wallet in the top drawer of the nightstand. The top drawer of his bureau would have his three sterling silver bracelets, one a family heirloom.

In Stone's closet, all his shirts were separated, long sleeved on one side, short sleeved on the other. They were subdivided by a dazzling array of color. Black and more black. There was one white shirt for the rare times that he needed to dress up. He owned a dark suit and had exactly two ties to choose from.

Jeans were stacked on a shelf. Workout shorts and swim trunks were folded with military precision on another.

Imaginative.

After helping himself to a pair of jeans and a T-shirt, Nate took a bite out of the crisp sour apple and put his own gun on the dresser top. He ignored the laundry hamper and dropped his wet clothes right in the middle of the bedroom floor to make a statement.

He took his time in the oversize shower. Stone's place was better than any hotel Nate had ever stayed in, reminding him of the luxurious Royal Sterling Hotel in Las Vegas. Nothing was overstated. Everything was elegant. Tiled floor with radiant heat, granite countertops—only the best for Wolf Stone.

Nate set the showerhead for a gentle spray, turning it from the "invigorating" pulse Stone had it set for.

The bar of soap sitting in the dish had a spicy, outdoorsy scent. Nate preferred something subtler. Something that smelled clean, maybe like a rainstorm. Still, beggars couldn't be choosers.

He shampooed.

He stalled.

He soaped again.

He waited.

"You know where the guest room is."

Score.

"And the hamper."

The glass door wasn't steamed over, meaning Stone could see exactly what Nate was doing. So he took time lathering his balls, making sure to wash them thoroughly. Then he drew upward on his cock.

"You're pushing your luck, Davidson. I'll put you back out in the weather so fucking fast—"

"Stone?" Nate turned off the faucet and pulled open the door. "Shut up."

Stone's jaw slackened.

Nate knew he'd pay for the comment later, so he enjoyed the hell out of the shocked moment while it lasted. "Forgot to grab a towel."

Stone snatched a white towel from a well-organized basket and tossed it at Nate.

"Thanks." Instead of wrapping it around his waist, he dried his face and hair, ignoring the rest of his body.

Stone stood there, unmoving.

Even when they were apart, Nate fantasized about having Stone's cock up his ass. It didn't matter who he was with, where he found his release—it was Stone he thought of, Stone he wanted.

Now that they were together, Nate wouldn't be put off again.

He wanted Stone, and Stone wanted him. Could the math get any simpler?

From their past experience, he knew the alpha male wouldn't be gentle when it happened. Stone would take Nate the way he wanted to be taken, hard and fast, possessively.

He just wanted it to happen sooner, not later.

Stone didn't leave the bathroom, and tension grew taut and stretched. Nate did nothing to defuse it.

"Why did you volunteer?"

"Hawkeye thinks you need backup, and you refused his offer of help. So a few of us are using our personal time."

"Waste of vacation hours, if you ask me."

"I didn't. None of us consider it a waste of our time. You'd do the same for any one of us." And had, on many occasions. "The threat's real, Stone. You have to know that."

"It won't happen here."

"It could."

"They want me on their turf."

And it went without saying that Stone would take the battle to them. When he did, Nate would be at his side. He'd defend this man to the death.

"You disobeyed a direct order to leave the premises."

"Yeah," Nate agreed. Even though the air in the bathroom was cooling, his cock stayed hard. He was so aroused he could jump from his skin.

"I don't take that lightly."

Under Stone's penetrating stare, Nate lowered his gaze. It wasn't in apology. It was in stark recognition of the other man's authority.

Before he knew what was happening, Stone had acted, tossing the towel to the floor.

Stone spun Nate, wrenching his arm up his back. "Fuck!" He gasped.

Stone moved in closer, slamming Nate's pelvis into the counter. Nate struggled, but it didn't matter. Despite his injury, Stone subdued Nate as if he were a rank amateur instead of a trained professional. An unsubtle reminder of who was boss.

He breathed deeply, and after a few seconds, Stone eased his grip.

"Still think I can't take care of myself?"

"Never said you couldn't," Nate said. "Just here to watch your back." Aware of the scratch of denim, and the brutal hardness of Stone's cock, Nate met the larger man's eyes in the mirror. God, he wanted him. Wanted him so bad.

"Spread your legs."

Nate could have died on the spot.

"Now."

As best he could, trapped as he was, he spread his legs.

"I should fuck you hard without preparation. Make you take me."

The threat turned Nate on. But it would never happen. Stone wasn't that much of an asshole.

Stone reached around Nate to open a drawer.

Lube. And a condom.

Nate closed his eyes.

"Look at me," Stone commanded. "I want to see exactly what you're thinking."

As difficult as it was to comply, Nate did as ordered. He just wanted to surrender to the sensations. But Stone wanted him as an active participant.

One-handed, Stone flipped the top and squirted a dollop onto the countertop.

Even above the sound of his own ragged breathing, Nate heard Stone's zipper. Then he eased back a bit, probably to lower his jeans.

"What do you want?" Stone asked.

"You." Nate's arm was wrenched a bit higher. "Your cock," he clarified around a gasp.

Stone used his left hand and his teeth to rip open the condom's wrapper.

Could this take any longer? His patience was fried. He didn't intend to wait another five stinking minutes.

Stone put on the condom.

"I'm clean," Nate said.

"So am I. But we'll do it my way until we have the chance to talk." Stone then scooped some of the lube from the granite.

Nate tensed when the cool gel was smeared on his anus. "Give me your finger!"

Stone did.

Nate gasped at the sudden intrusion. *Christ.*

Stone stretched him, lubed him, shoved deep inside. He rose onto his toes as Stone dominated him.

Then Stone's cockhead pressed against the barely stretched opening. Even though Nate had been lubed and prepped, he wasn't ready for someone as big, as rigid, as Stone. "It's been a long time for me," Nate said, by way of plea.

"You should have thought about that before you goaded me." Stone bit his ear.

Nate cried out in pleasure and arched his back.

Stone drove his cock home.

Nate was stretched, invaded, hurting.

This was about punishment, Nate knew. But it was about a whole lot more as well. This was pent-up frustration.

Stone found his own rhythm, deep, slamming against Nate's prostate. He'd never felt anything this overwhelming. He was consumed with it, by it. So close…so close to his own orgasm.

"Don't even think of touching your cock."

He'd been considering exactly that. But now, forbidden even that, he had no option but to surrender to Stone's punishing thrusts.

Stone clamped down on Nate's shoulder, his fingers

digging into the flesh. With a grunt, he came. The feeling of his Dominant coming inside him made Nate shudder. There was nothing he wanted more.

And even though Nate had been denied his own orgasm, he was totally satisfied.

Their gazes collided in the mirror again.

Nate saw the same raw desire in the alpha male's eyes that he knew was reflected in his own.

Deliberately, no motion wasted, Stone untangled their bodies. He started by releasing his grip on Nate's shoulder, then his arm. Finally, Stone eased his cock from Nate's ass.

"Your cock still hard?" Instead of waiting for an answer, Stone reached around and felt for himself.

Blood flooded Nate's entire body where circulation returned. And his penis was full-length, turgid. He moaned when Stone stroked him. "Yes!" God, what would it be like to once again receive a hand job from his alpha? "Stone…"

"If I keep doing this, are you going to come?"

"I…" He tipped his head back. "Yes."

Stone stopped his motions. "Get dressed and meet us in the great room."

Nate sagged, catching himself against the counter. "Finish me off!"

"Get dressed." Stone's voice was as cold as the weather.

"Bastard."

"If you jerk off, I'll know."

He would, too.

"And if you do, your punishment will mean you don't get my cock later. Understand?"

Miserable, Nate nodded.

The bedroom door slammed behind Stone.

Nate had finally gotten what he wanted. The man he desired above all others had taken him, used him like he had before, rode him, punished him, like he needed.

After such a long absence, the taste wasn't enough.

Damn. Damn. Fuck it all.

He strode to Stone's bed and snatched up the jeans he'd selected.

Even though he could ejaculate in under a dozen strokes, he knew the same thing that Stone knew. Because he'd issued a direct order, Nate wouldn't touch himself.

———

JUMPING OUT OF HER SKIN, KAYLA PLACED HER EMPTY wineglass on the kitchen counter. She'd do anything to know what the two men were up to in the bedroom. But Stone, damn him, had shut the door behind him.

That hadn't stopped her from listening, though. The masculine grunts and cries had whetted her appetite.

She considered herself a progressive type of person. In fact, some of her friends, female as well as male, were gay. But she hadn't ever given much thought to what they actually did when the lights went out.

Until now.

The image of Stone with his cock up Nate's ass made her pussy wet. But how the hell was she supposed to ask if she could watch them the next time they had sex?

She was considering a second glass of wine when Stone strode in.

He filled the space, stole her breath. She couldn't believe it, but she wanted him, probably now more than ever, and that confused the hell out of her. How could she desire a man who'd just primitively taken another man?

"I'll have one of those," he said, indicating the uncorked bottle.

She nodded. Her hand shook a bit as she poured. "So..."

Since the word sounded wobbly, she cleared her throat. "About what just happened..."

"Your face is the same color as the merlot," he observed as she offered him the glass of wine.

"Yes, well..." She blushed often, much to her chagrin. Throughout her childhood, she'd been teased mercilessly. After handing off the stemware, she fanned her face.

The rain still beat a nasty staccato against the window-panes, and the fire in the great room had turned to embers.

She backed up against the counter and spread her arms, gripping the edge as if she didn't have a care in the world. Truthfully, her heart pounded so hard she wondered if it would explode. "I'm curious."

He took an appreciative sip of the room-temperature merlot. "Go on."

"Nate said neither of you are strictly homosexual."

"We're not."

"As long as you can be the dominant one?"

He took a drink and regarded her over the rim. "Is this a clinical question, or a personal one?"

"I couldn't help but hear—"

"Because you were eavesdropping," he interrupted. "You're blushing again."

Aware of the message her body language was sending, she folded her arms protectively across her chest.

"You couldn't help but hear..." Stone prompted.

"And I want to watch."

"You'd rather watch two men get it on than participate?"

"Participate?" She blinked. "Like with the *two* of you?" Maybe she was mistaken. Maybe he didn't mean anything of the sort. "Like a *threesome*?"

"Or some variation," he said.

How the hell could there be a variation? She wasn't exactly naive, but maybe he needed to draw her a picture.

More quietly, intimately, he went on. "Have you ever been dominated, Fagan? Sexually dominated?"

"No. But…I've seen your room in the basement."

"The whips? The Saint Andrew's cross?"

The eroticism in his words buzzed through her head.

"Have you ever been submissive? Knelt? Fetched a paddle? Served your Dominant's pleasure?"

"No." She gulped.

"And you're curious."

Her mind exploded with images of being with him. She nodded.

"Just so I understand you explicitly, I want answers. Honest ones. Am I clear?"

The intensity in his eyes shot tension through her. "Yes, Wolf."

"Good. A submissive is expected to participate, to draw the boundaries, to be unflinchingly candid about what he or she wants. That's what I demand from anyone who submits to me."

Was she going to do that? Submit to him? Put her trust in his hands? Tell him what she wanted? "I want to explore," she confessed.

"Why?"

Unflinchingly candid. "I want to experience the vulnerability. The honesty."

"Honesty?"

"I'm tired of running and hiding."

"Tell me more."

Kayla uncrossed her arms then dug her fingernails into her palms for courage. "I've always wanted more." She paused. Silence stretched, as if it were a physical thing. "I mean sexually. It's been okay, but… I don't know. Lacking the connection I thought it would have." Maybe it was her, the awful experiences she'd had with her husband. But now that Stone was demanding that she confront her needs, she was more aroused than she'd been in years...if ever.

"Have you pictured yourself spread open wide begging for my lash?"

He left her breathless.

"You are now, aren't you, Fagan? Wondering? It will hurt. Despite that, maybe because of that, you want it. And the idea of being with two men intrigues you."

"Yes." The images made her tremble. "I want to be shattered. I want to be so complete, so satisfied that I'm not able to make a grocery list in my head after sex."

"Grocery lists? You've been having sex with the wrong men," Nate said.

She blinked. She hadn't realized Nate was in the room.

He pushed away from the wall and walked toward them. "Is Kayla coming on to you, Stone?"

"Seems she wants to dance with danger." Wolf raised his glass in her direction. Then he looked back at Nate. "You opposed to eating pussy?"

Kayla blinked. She couldn't possibly have heard correctly.

Nate shrugged. "I've done it once or twice."

"You any good at it?"

"I've never had any complaints."

Wolf put down his wineglass. "Get on your knees, Davidson."

With mesmerizing grace, Nate followed his Dominant's command.

"What will it be, Fagan?" Wolf asked over the kneeling man's head. "Do you want to take a walk where you've never gone before? It won't always be what you want or what you expect. But it will always be good for you."

When Stone suggested they play together, she'd pictured the two of them in the basement, her tied up, him making her come over and over again until she was exhausted. She hadn't been prepared for Stone to order Nate to pleasure her orally.

"What will it be, Fagan?"

She tamped down her jitters in favor of the thrill of living fully. "Yes. I want this."

Stone nodded tightly. "Keep your eyes on me. And strip from the waist down."

CHAPTER THREE

HAWKEYE

Be careful what you wish for. Hadn't she used that as a motto her entire life?

Now that she was faced with the reality, she was terrified. Instead of one man, she had two. Nate was on his knees, waiting for her. And Wolf held her gaze pinned in a dangerous game of dominance and submission.

Even though she wasn't sure she was actually going to go through with it, she reached for the top snap on her jeans. "I need another drink of wine."

He shook his head. "I want you clearheaded."

"Impossible with the two of you here." She smiled, but he didn't return it.

"I have no tolerance for prevarication."

His eyes mesmerized, his voice hypnotized.

He kept his gaze on her as she followed his orders.

Usually, she hurried through the undressing part, and she generally had the lights off. And now she was stripping in broad daylight, in the kitchen, in front of two men.

She removed her shoes and socks, then wiggled out of her jeans before kicking aside the denim. She wore a pretty, feminine pair of underwear with little bows near her hipbones.

"Nice." The purr in Wolf's voice sent warm skitters through her. "Take them off."

Fortunately, trimming her pubic area was a daily practice. She started to cover herself but then stopped. Instead, she let her arms dangle next to her body.

His eyes darkened with approval, and that helped her swallow her embarrassment.

"Have you ever had your cunt licked while another man watched? Look at me!"

She shook her head and returned her gaze to his face. "No." Her stomach was a massive knot of nerves. Had Nate gone through the same thing when Wolf snapped orders and then fucked him so hard that he cried out?

"You can stop anytime. I understand it may be too much for you."

His voice, now oddly compassionate, spoke to something deep inside her, inviting trust. "I'm okay."

"Good. In that case, turn around. When you have, spread your legs as far apart as you can, then grab your ankles."

Her mouth was dry. He knew exactly what he was asking. Before Nate tongued her, she'd have to expose herself to both men.

Instead of reissuing the command, Wolf waited. Knowing it was completely up to her whether she complied or not, she took a deep steadying breath.

Her turn wasn't as elegant as she would have liked, but neither man commented.

She held onto her ankles. Her hair hung down, all but brushing the floor. Unable to believe she was doing this, Kayla closed her eyes.

"Spread your labia for us." Wolf's voice flowed with silken sensuality.

Now that the embarrassment was fading, doing what he said was easier.

Within moments, she was opened wide. Exposed. Vulnerable. Was there anything more intimate?

"Beautiful."

That came from Nate. And from this upside-down position, she had a good view of his knees.

"You are aroused," Wolf observed.

"I'm getting there."

"Davidson, do a little exploration. Figure out what she likes."

In that moment, she understood a lot more about dominance and submission. Nate didn't hesitate as he moved in, settling his hands on her thighs.

She quivered.

And she remembered the way Nate had dropped to his knees without protest when Stone told him to. It really didn't matter if he liked to eat pussy or not. He would do it regardless, because Stone said so and he was the Dominant.

"Be sure to stay in position for me," Nate instructed.

Two of them. Two men telling her what to do. Two of them showing encouragement and demanding her obedience.

With his fingers, his mouth impossibly close, Nate teased her, making her delirious. "Lick me!" *Please.*

"Anything you wish." He swept his tongue from back to front, starting at her ass, crossing her vagina, and then up her clit.

Her knees buckled, pitching her forward.

"Grab your ankles again, Fagan." To Nate, he added, "I think she liked that."

"Yes." She inhaled. "Yes, I liked that."

"Do not come," Wolf said, "until I give you permission."

"What?" She was gasping, wiggling, wanting more.

"My game. My rules. Would you like to play or not?"

Nate circled her clit, uncoiling the first waves of an orgasm deep inside her. She angled her hips, silently asking for more.

"Fagan?"

Nate stopped entirely.

She pushed herself upright as quickly as she could and spun around to face both of them. Bastards! "Damn it!" She glared at Wolf, sparing him none of her wrath. "Damn you."

Like the lord and master of the manor, he folded his arms. His blue eyes blazed with intensity. "I warned you it wouldn't always be what you want."

Half-naked, her clit throbbing in an insistent demand, she was at a disadvantage.

"What's it to be?" he asked.

"You get to control my..." She nearly sputtered. "My orgasms?"

"Only if you want to scene with me."

"And me," Nate added.

"You're both impossible."

"And you are bad-tempered." Wolf was unyielding. "Probably because you're sexually frustrated."

"There is that."

"This is about you granting me power while learning to control your own reactions to prolong the pleasure. If you want to go on, quit fighting."

Damn it. It was what she wanted. Slowly, she nodded. "Yes," she whispered.

"Get back into position."

Kayla turned around, spread her legs, then bent to expose herself like Wolf expected.

"Good girl."

She waited and waited. When she nearly gave up hope, Wolf finally broke the silence. "Davidson, you may proceed."

Nate came in closer to he could lick her slowly, as if savoring her taste. Then he drew her clit into his mouth and pressed on it with his tongue.

Undulating, she gasped, and an orgasm nipped at her insides.

"Control yourself, Fagan." Wolf's words were wrapped in warning.

She wanted him, wanted both of them.

"Direct your concentration elsewhere," he encouraged.

Kayla wondered if that would work when she had his cock in her mouth and he was ready to orgasm. She couldn't wait to pull away and suggest he restrain himself.

She struggled to do as he said, and it became more and more difficult as Nate sucked on her, nibbled on her, licked her.

"Keep your attention on me," Wolf encouraged.

Nate continued to pleasure her orally, then, when she wasn't expecting it, he inserted a finger into her pussy. She cried out. "I need…"

In and out. He simulated the sex act, and she was nearly undone, knowing that Wolf was not only watching, he was orchestrating the entire scene.

"Please."

"A few more seconds."

There was no way to hold on. She couldn't concentrate long enough to remember to breathe. She'd never been this out of control. Gasping, panting, the world careened around her.

"Now."

Ruthlessly, Nate plunged a second finger in her.

She screamed as her pussy clenched and a climax rocked her.

The orgasm was more intense than anything she'd ever experienced, and her body went limp.

Wolf was there to catch her. Gratefully, she surrendered into the comfort his arms. Then, moments later, when he sought her mouth, her emotions fractured. Since her husband's death, she hadn't been kissed. "Oh, oh." She laced her hands around his neck as he offered comfort and tenderness, then slowly coaxed her response until he consumed her.

She'd never experienced anything like it. It was potent and addictive. "More." She wanted more.

"Insatiable wench," Nate teased.

They had no idea...

CHAPTER FOUR

HAWKEYE

"How about pizza?" Wolf asked.

"I'm ravenous." The adrenaline from her introduction to BDSM had faded, leaving Kayla drained. After their scene, the men had helped her to get dressed again, but she was still trying to find her equilibrium. "I think we still have a feta cheese and sun dried tomato one in the freezer."

"How about pepperoni?"

"They're all gone. Mrs. Johnson wants us to get some fruits and veggies in our diet."

"A man needs meat," he protested. "I'm going to fire her."

"You're both heathens." Nate shuddered, then opened the refrigerator door. "Kayla, set the table and pour some wine. Stone, go do whatever it is you do in your Batcave, and I'll cook something decent."

"I suppose you think you're staying?" Stone asked.

"I am."

"You weren't invited," Stone reminded him.

"Didn't expect to be."

"You could still leave."

"I could. Then you'd have frozen pizza for dinner."

"Again," Kayla supplied.

"You can stay through dinner."

"Big of you."

What the hell was it between the two of them? Obviously they'd had some sort of relationship in the past. Stone was a man of few—but sincere—words, so she didn't think he'd been making casual conversation when he said he hadn't wanted Nate there. And he *had* left him out in the weather...

As Nate defrosted steaks, he threw together a salad and warmed a loaf of French bread.

Kayla happily helped, despite her lack of domestic skills. She knew how to turn on the microwave, fry eggs in a pile of bacon grease, brew coffee in a percolator over a campfire, hotwire a car with her eyes closed, could bandage up someone good enough to get them to an extraction point, but blending homemade salad dressing was out of reach.

"This kitchen is wasted on Stone," Nate lamented, turning on the stove's grill feature. He adjusted the gas jets until the flames suited him.

"He had the house built," she reminded him.

"Because the designer convinced him it would have a higher resale value with a fabulous kitchen."

"And just how is it that someone who's highly trained in search and rescue knows how to prepare a gourmet meal out of a handful of ingredients?"

"Just because I can rappel from a helicopter to save your butt doesn't mean I don't have taste buds. And I'm good at improvisation, no matter the situation." He popped a radish in his mouth. "Thank God someone stocks his refrigerator."

Mrs. Johnson was amazing. She came in once a week, brought fresh food, and fussed over Stone—well, as much as he'd let anyone fuss over him. Kayla's jaw had dropped when the older woman actually pinched his cheek and called him Wolfie.

"Don't you dare try it," he'd warned Kayla.

Still, despite the woman's earnest efforts, Kayla and Wolf had made do with cereal for breakfast, sandwiches for lunch, and something frozen for dinner. She considered her sandwich gourmet when it had fancy mustard on it.

She decided on the second glass of wine after all. It had been an odd day. Wasn't often, or ever, that one man licked her from front to back while another watched and gave instructions.

Had it really happened?

Because the wine loosened her a bit, she was emboldened. "What happened earlier," she said. "I enjoyed that." Heat flooding her face, she looked down.

"Stone has that effect on people."

"I wasn't talking about him. You're a very sexy guy, Nate Davidson."

He shook the colander to drain the lettuce. "You're not too bad yourself." He grinned, and her insides melted a bit. "I liked your reactions. I think maybe I've been missing out, not eating you out before now."

What was happening here?

That she was attracted to Stone, the enigmatic leader, wasn't a surprise. But that she was getting emotionally sideways over two men...? She shook her head. She was entering dangerous—forbidden—territory.

Nate put the steaks on the grill, searing the meat. A few minutes later, Stone joined them. He picked up his earlier glass of wine.

"Everything okay in the Batcave?" Nate asked.

"No more of my teammates have been caught trespassing, if that's what you're asking."

Rather than respond, Nate changed the subject. "How do you like your steak, boss? Rare?"

"Is there any other way?"

"A man after my heart," Nate said.

"I have no interest in your heart, Davidson."

Nate turned and grinned. "I had hoped something else was more interesting."

She realized she hadn't yet seen either of them naked. And this so wasn't fair. It was like being given a taste of dessert, then told she couldn't have the rest of the cake.

Nate served the food. As if it was his right, Wolf sat at the head of the table, she and Nate on either side of him.

An appreciative Wolf took a bite of his T-bone. "Maybe you can stay a bit longer."

"I thought you'd never ask."

"So where does that leave Ms. Fagan?" Wolf put down his knife and fork. "Who is here, apparently, under false pretenses."

The food suddenly tasted like ash in her mouth. "I'm trained to help with your physical therapy." So it wasn't *exactly* false pretenses.

"And what else?"

"I can shoot."

"Don't let her fool you. She's one of Hawkeye's best. He wouldn't send anyone less. We all know it."

"How'd you get involved?"

"Long story," she replied.

"We've got time." Wolf gave no quarter. She was in his home, and in his eyes, she'd lied her way in.

She'd barely been tolerated when he thought she was a physical therapist. Now that he knew she was assigned to protection...? She shifted. "Look, I—"

"You don't have to tell us anything," Nate interrupted. "Los Angeles made a believer out of me."

Stone continued to sit there, regarding her with steely eyes.

"I was married at twenty-two. To a cop. And of course, I

went to the police academy." Pain traced a familiar path through her heart. "My husband got caught in a drug deal gone bad." Few people knew the story of her past, and she hated sharing it.

Stone frowned. "He was working undercover?"

"No." She twirled the globe of her wineglass between her palms. "He was dirty." She exhaled. "I'd known he had a problem, but he said it was in the past. I believed him when he said he was clean."

Without judgment, Stone nodded.

"He died of multiple gunshot wounds."

"That's harsh," Nate said.

"I quit the force." She dragged her hair back. "People looked at me with suspicion, as if I'd known. As if I had something to do with it. I was investigated in case I was bad too." Not only had she lost her husband, her ideals about him had been destroyed. Her devastation had plunged her into a downward spiral, and the memory of it left her raw and embarrassed. If a friend hadn't suggested she apply at Hawkeye Security, and if Hawkeye's right-hand woman, Inamorata, hadn't taken a chance on her, Kayla wasn't sure where she'd be now.

"I've been with you in the field. You're a damn fine agent." Nate was loyal, always. "Your PD lost a good officer."

She gave a half smile, attempting to shove the memories away where she could lock them up.

"I have no doubt you're good. You'd have washed out if you weren't," Stone agreed. "Your situation would have clobbered anyone. You did good."

She'd pried open a part of her heart to expose her deepest secrets, and both men had her back. Relief combined with gratitude and settled in to become deep affection for them.

For the next few minutes, they ate in silence. When Wolf spoke again, she knew things were back on even terrain.

"So, we've ascertained you're both excellent operatives. Tell me, do I look like I need a babysitter?"

Saying nothing, Nate took a sip of water, leaving her to flounder.

"Your range of motion isn't what it should be." Undaunted, she returned Wolf's stare.

He raised a brow. "I had no trouble subduing Davidson."

"Because he isn't hell-bent on killing you," she fired back. Her anger flared. More than anyone, he knew what it meant to go up against Huffman. Five years ago, he'd almost been brought to trial for his extortion and Ponzi schemes. But when the prosecution's star witness ended up dead, his head in a different trash can than his bullet-riddled body, the case had been dismissed. She didn't want Wolf to be next. "If nothing else, maybe you could respect the fact we care about you and cooperate at least a little. You're an ungrateful bastard, Wolf Stone." She pushed back from the table. "Thanks for the food, Nate."

"Sit down," Stone said, his voice like a whiplash.

"With all due respect," which she didn't mean, she said, "screw you," which she did mean. "I'm here because I really, really believed that getting you healthy and keeping you alive is a good thing. But I'll tell you this—life taught me the fucking hard way that I can't help someone who doesn't want to be helped. I'll do my job." She leaned forward. "Do yours."

"She's right, you know. Trust is a two-way street."

"Not from you too," Stone said. What the hell did a man have to do to get some peace and quiet in his own house? He wanted to be left alone, which was why he was on eight hundred acres of hostile Rocky Mountain wilderness, surrounded by barbed wire and protected with the finest electronic security system known to man.

Except for the time he'd allowed Nate to visit, Stone hadn't sent out a single invitation to his house. In fact, only a handful of people knew where he lived.

Getting injured had pissed him off, but he'd been damn fortunate nothing vital had been hit.

Too bad that the shot he'd taken hadn't permanently taken out Michael Huffman. So now the cockroach was pissed. As if Stone hadn't had bad guys pissed at him before. "I can handle Huffman."

"If you were fully functional, you could." Nate leaned forward. "Self-reliance has its advantages." More quietly, he added, "So does working as a team."

"While you're here, you're not protecting people who really need it."

"There's a bounty out on you, and it's big enough to attract all sorts of mercenaries. *You're* the one who really needs it."

"Davidson—"

He shoved away from the table, his chair scooting along the polished hardwood floor. "You owe Kayla an apology for being an ass."

"An apology?"

"Yeah. Like where you say you're sorry. And you try to make it up to her."

"She lied to me."

"She's here because Hawkeye sent her. You've been sent plenty of places where people needed you but didn't want you." He grabbed an empty platter. "And she does have a delicious cunt."

Nate strode from the room.

Well. *Fuck.*

In the distance, a clock ticked off the seconds. Wind still howled and battered the house.

Davidson was right on most scores.

Trust *was* a two-way street. Maybe he'd do better if he'd stop being stubborn. Hawkeye Security hammered home the idea that no man was better alone than with a team.

And Fagan *did* have a nice cunt.

Thinking of her made his cock hard.

She'd been under his roof for several weeks, and he'd wanted her since the first time he set eyes on her, with her prim and proper button-down blouse, pulled-back hair, and lips with only the barest hint of gloss. Her black slacks had been a bit tight, and when she'd bent to pick something up, they'd stretched invitingly across her ass. He'd imagined his hands on her hips, imprisoning her while he filled her full of his cock.

And then Davidson had shown up as well.

Two sexy specimens, both willing to do his bidding.

Life could be a whole lot worse.

Stone massaged the ache in his leg. It had started with his knee, but it now traveled up his thigh. No matter what he tried to tell everyone, including himself, he wasn't one hundred percent operational. He'd navigated the mountain earlier, but not with the sure-footedness he normally did. He'd slipped on a wet rock, and when he caught himself, raw pain shot through him, instantly cramping the muscle. After getting back, he'd swallowed three or four ibuprofen, not that he'd admit it to Davidson or Fagan.

He went into the great room to find her there, stoking the fire. "Davidson says I should apologize."

She looked up from where she was crouched. "What do you think?"

"He's right. I'm an ass. You're putting yourself at risk, and I should respect that."

Her eyes lightened, and her shoulders rounded.

She let out a breath, indicating she was on her way to forgiving him.

"I'm not good at being protected. For you, I'll try."

Her soft sigh indicated she was on her way to forgiving him. "Wolf…"

"But I think I should spank your ass for your dishonesty."

Her mouth formed a shocked but delectable O. "I think I'll settle for the apology."

He laughed. "I didn't ask what you wanted." He took a couple of steps toward her. "And if you were honest, you'd admit that you'd really prefer the spanking."

"I…" She stood. "Hmm…"

"You've had apologies. But you've probably never had a spanking."

"You're right."

Her contradictions were beautiful. She wanted him to think she was prim and proper, but prim and proper ladies didn't look him in the eye and tell him to screw off. They didn't put on a slicker and head out into the wilderness to find a fellow operative. "And until this afternoon, you'd never dropped your pants in the kitchen and had one man tongue you to orgasm while another watched."

"Well, there is that."

"It's up to you," he said.

"Where, theoretically, would this spanking happen?"

"Right here." He rolled up the sleeves of his shirt. "Right now." He watched emotions play across her face. A frown of concern. Then a little twist of her lips as she contemplated his offer.

"Over my clothes?"

"I've already seen your naked butt."

In the reflection of the firelight, her green eyes had flecks of copper. "This spanking. Would it be with your hand?"

She was reading him correctly. The spanking wasn't an end—it was the doorway to exploring her fantasies. So, the only question was, did she have the guts to really go for it? "We can work up to other implements later, if you think you can handle it."

"Was that a challenge?"

He damn near grinned.

"How many?" she asked, unfastening the top button of her jeans once again. "Spanks?"

"Two dozen."

Her hand froze. "Two *dozen?*"

"Unless you beg me to keep going."

"Close your mouth," Nate said from the doorway. He was rubbing lotion into his hands, and he joined them in the great room. "If you ever have any hope of getting to play on his cross, you have to start somewhere."

"I apologized to her," Stone said.

"Good. Which will make the spanking all that much better," Nate agreed.

"In that case, get in line."

"I'm happy to be first, boss."

In the fireplace, a log popped and hissed.

"You mean..." Kayla glanced between the two men before settling on Nate's grin. "You're not just bisexual, but you like to be spanked?"

"I told you to stop letting your mouth fall open like that." Nate placed his forefinger beneath her chin and pushed up. "And, yes. I adore it. Stone's a hell of a Dominant."

Stone enjoyed the interplay between the two of them, and he loved seeing her shocked. He adjusted his jeans to make room for his hardening cock.

"On second thought, maybe I shouldn't be first. We might scare her."

"You've got a hard ass," Stone agreed. "And you'll be

starting with something a lot more substantial than my hand."

"I want to watch," she said stubbornly.

That was a start.

Stone nodded. "Downstairs. Both of you."

CHAPTER FIVE

HAWKEYE

Kayla couldn't believe this.

Her mouth was dry, and her palms were damp. She was going to watch Stone spank Nate. Dread and excitement warred in her.

Stone pushed open the door to his secret room and indicated she should precede them.

Now that she was inside, knowing she'd also have a turn, everything was so much more real, so much more threatening.

She would have waited for instructions, but Nate didn't. He seemed eager to please, happy to be on with it.

He took off his T-shirt and folded it.

Oh God. He was a hunk and a half. He obviously worked out, and his muscles were well-defined and honed. She'd never had a lover as sexy as him. All he needed was some oil smeared on him, and he'd be good for a magazine shoot. Well, apart from the jagged scar along his rib cage. But that only made him more appealing. Too much perfection wasn't a good thing.

She stole a glance at Stone.

He'd crossed to the far wall, and he was taking down some sort of evil-looking leather implement.

He was actually going to use that on Nate?

Suddenly, she needed to sit.

In the corner, there was a bench that resembled the ones she trained on at the gym. With relief, she lowered herself onto it. Neither man seemed to notice her.

Stone put the torture device back, and she let out a breath she hadn't realized she'd been holding.

Nate dropped his pants—seemed he rarely wore shoes in the house—and he had nothing underneath. His pubic hair was trimmed, and his cock was partially aroused. He folded his borrowed jeans and placed them on top of the T-shirt.

"You sure you're up for this?" Stone asked.

In silent response, Nate knelt.

Was she expected to behave like that?

Tension settled over the room, and her heart drummed in her ears.

"Over there." Stone hooked his thumb toward the middle of the room.

Nate crawled to a piece of equipment that reminded her of a gymnast's pommel horse. This apparatus had several sturdy pieces of leather attached to it. For ankles and wrists, she assumed.

Nate draped himself over the top, and Stone asked, "Would you like to be tied?"

"The choice is yours, boss. Always."

The more she observed, the more she questioned her ability to be good at this.

"Wrists only," Stone said.

Nate spread his arms wide.

"Fagan, secure him."

She glanced around, as if expecting some other Kayla to leap into action.

"*Now*, Fagan." The command was half growl, half bark.

Jolted, she hurried over to Nate. "I'm sorry," she said, feeling slightly disloyal as she fastened the buckles.

"Don't be."

His satisfied smile shocked her.

"Give me a safe word, Davidson."

"Red." Nate paused. "I won't be using it."

"Spread your legs a couple more inches."

Her mouth was dry. Wolf was a harsh Dominant. But Nate's expression never changed. He just maneuvered until Stone told him to stop.

As Wolf adjusted the horse higher, Nate grunted. He was forced onto his toes, and his body was stretched a little more uncomfortably.

His cock wasn't as thick as it had been.

Wolf crouched near the piece of equipment, his movement slow and awkward. No doubt he'd reinjured himself on the mountainside.

Moving forward, he took Nate's balls in his palm, as if weighing them.

Nate moaned.

"Would you like a gag?"

"Only if it pleases you, boss. Sorry for the outburst."

Stone tugged down a bit, and Nate again moaned.

"Repeat your safe word, Davidson."

She wondered if this was a usual part of the way he played with his...subs. Each motion was leaderlike.

Since he had a room filled with toys and equipment, dominance and submission had to be an integral part of Wolf's personality. Anyone getting involved with him would not only have to accept that, they'd probably have to participate, and maybe on a regular basis, more than just an occasional diversion.

She swallowed hard, wondering what she'd gotten herself into, and more, wondering why she didn't want to get out.

"I'm waiting," Stone prompted.

"Red," Nate whispered.

"Would you like to use it?"

"No, boss." Nate shook his head.

"I'm going to squeeze your testicles, Davidson."

He got no response.

"And then I'm going to roll them between my palms. I will be deliberate. But I won't go easy on you."

"Yes, boss."

"You'll feel the pain all the way up in your abdomen."

She was nervous on Nate's behalf. "Uh…"

"He can stop the play at any time," Stone told her. "What do you want me to do, Davidson?"

"Tell Fagan to mind her own business."

He was actually *enjoying* this?

On unsteady legs, she returned to the bench. Better than her knees collapsing and dropping her on her ass.

"It's called CBT for short." Never looking her direction, Wolf continued to explain. "Cock and ball torture. It's nothing we haven't explored before. A lot of male subs like it. And having him submit to it pleases me. I pulled down first, to get his testicles taut in the bottom of the sac."

"I'm glad I don't have balls."

He glanced over his shoulder with a terrible smile. It did nothing to reassure her and everything to unleash a spike of adrenaline-laced fear down her spine.

"I know all about nipple and tit torture too."

"You know about…?" Oh God. Her breasts throbbed as unholy fascination teased her libido.

"In the next twenty minutes, you're going to learn all about it too." The lines of his face were set in an implacable mask.

Her stomach flip-flopped.

"Your nipples will be clamped. What do you say, Davidson? Will she look better in clover clamps or alligator ones?"

"The D-shaped ones," Nate said.

"You're right," Wolf agreed.

Then he seemed to totally forget about her, even though she was left reeling. She couldn't imagine being tied up, her nipples squeezed by torturous clamps. And yet... Yet she watched him so skillfully master Nate. There was pain, but he liked it. She'd be asked for a safe word too. Nothing would happen that she refused to participate in. Despite her apprehension, she knew she wouldn't refuse.

Kayla twisted her hands together. Realizing she was betraying her nerves, she kept still, even as Stone rolled the trapped balls in his large palms.

Nate whimpered.

"Back and forth." Stone's voice was smooth, almost hypnotic. "You're doing well. You're pleasing me."

"Yes." The word was hissed through Nate's clenched teeth.

"Keep your legs parted. Unless you'd like Fagan to tie you?"

Nate struggled back into position.

"Is it too much?"

Nate shook his head.

"Then ask for more pressure."

She crossed her legs in mute sympathy.

"I..."

"Ask me," Wolf said softly.

"More. Make it hurt more."

"Yeah. My pleasure."

Stone exerted more pressure. There was nothing rough or jerky in his motions. In fact, he used exquisite precision.

Nate rocked onto his toes.

"More?"

"N...No."

"Just five more."

"Yes, boss."

Stone backed off the tension, even as he rolled Nate's balls in between his palms with great care.

Nate's ragged breathing returned to normal after a few deep gulps. "Thank you." His hoarse voice was barely audible.

"I wondered where your manners were."

"He has to thank you?" She rubbed her damp palms on her thighs.

"And so will you, Fagan."

Not likely.

He stood, then crossed in front of the horse to stroke Nate's hair. The tenderness made her yearn for love—a love she'd never had. What would it be like to be the center of her lover's universe? Having a man push her limits, giving her what she wanted before he tenderly touched her?

"Best I've ever had," Nate said.

"Not done with you."

"Did Kayla run away yet?"

"I think her shoes are glued to the floor."

"Beat me," Nate implored.

"My pleasure. Choose your implement."

She'd hung around her teammates long enough to know that their adrenaline craving drove them to danger. Extreme sports. Drinking. Why would sex be any different? None of them knew how much time they had together. Why save something for later?

Despite her nerves, Stone was right. She wanted to be here.

"You had a tawse in your hand."

"Fagan, grab him a bottle of water." Stone unfastened Nate, then rubbed his wrists. "I want you on the cross."

She looked around until she found a small refrigerator tucked into the corner. It was stocked with water and some sports drinks.

"Some Doms aren't as thoughtful as Stone," Nate said as Kayla opened the bottle and handed it to him.

He'd just had his balls squeezed in Stone's hands, and Stone was *thoughtful?*

He took a couple sips and handed it back.

"When you're ready," Stone said patiently, as if he had all the time in the world.

"Yeah." Nate nodded. I've got my bearings back." Without assistance, he walked to the cross, faced it, spread his legs, then his arms.

"You get Davidson's legs," Stone instructed. "I'll get his wrists."

This time, she had no qualms about following Stone's instructions.

Nate's cock stirred, arousing her.

She needed to talk to both men when this was over. In the reading she'd done, and in talking with a friend who practiced S&M, she had never realized all this ceremony and negotiation was involved. Every moment seemed to set the stage, enhance the experience. She had no doubt this was as much about Nate's pleasure as Wolf's. Her fear excited her, and she wanted to experience it for herself.

"I'll give you five as a warm-up," Stone said. "Before the twelve you deserve."

Nate nodded. "Thank you, boss."

"Want to join in?" Stone ensnared her gaze. "Stroke Davidson off during his beating."

"I might die," Nate said.

"That'd be convenient, since you'll already be in heaven," Stone shot back, apparently unconcerned. "Fagan?"

Kayla licked her lips. Dry mouth seemed to have become an occupational hazard.

"Do not touch him while I give him the first five."

Her heart thumped as if an anvil were inside.

"Then keep your eye on me. I'll nod when you're to begin and shake my head when you're to stop. And even if this naughty baggage begs you to keep going, act only upon my instructions."

"I understand."

"First the warm up." Stone he drew back and delivered five blows with the tawse.

Other than a slight moan, Nate had no reaction.

"You took those well." Wolf put on a pair of leather gloves and vigorously rubbed Nate's hindquarters.

His cock jumped. His body shuddered. "Boss? This will never encourage me to behave."

Wolf captured Kayla's gaze, and went to the cross. After picking up the tawse, he pulled back his hand and struck Nate under his right buttock.

She reached for his cock, only to have Wolf shake his head. She frowned. But just as quickly, he delivered a second smack on Nate's left buttock.

She closed her hand around Nate's cock. It hardened slightly.

"The boy likes it rough," Wolf said.

She tightened her grip and slid her hand all the way up Nate's cock, then down. Wolf allowed the ministration to go on for a few seconds before shaking his head.

Abruptly, she released her grip.

Although Nate sagged in his bonds, his cock stayed hard.

Without giving Nate time to recover, Stone delivered the next three strokes before nodding at her.

Understanding more now, she first licked her hand, then grasped Nate's dick and squeezed hard.

"That's it." Approval rippled through Wolf's voice. "Keep going."

When Nate sucked in a harsh breath, Wolf barked out his order to stop.

"Please, boss. Let her finish me."

"Is that a drop of precum on Davidson's cockhead?" Wolf asked.

She nodded.

Wolf himself moved in front of Nate and sucked on his cock.

Nate's motions were desperate. "I swear I'll do anything you want."

Pulling away, Wolf laughed. "I bet you will."

"Boss, I can't take more."

"Yeah. You can." Wolf continued. After the next smack made Nate jut his hips forward, she stroked him hard.

His cock was turgid, demanding. On her own, she would have kept going until he ejaculated.

"Good news, Davidson. You're halfway there. Fagan, remove your hand."

She pulled away.

A strangled word ripped from Nate's throat.

"You didn't just swear, did you?"

"No, boss!" His voice caught on a plaintive wail.

"Good," Wolf said. His seventh, eighth, and ninth spanks were delivered flat, across the fleshiest part of Nate's ass. Wolf didn't grant Nate any quarter. "Give him half a dozen long, slow strokes, will you, Fagan? Very light grip."

This was a complete turnaround from the frantic way she'd been jacking him off.

Through his whimpers, he whispered. "More, more, harder."

But she had her orders from Wolf. He was the one with the tawse.

"Tell Ms. Fagan thank you."

"Thank you," Nate whispered.

"Three to go." Wolf gave one stripe from the bottom, angled up. The second came harder. "Stroke him, but don't let him ejaculate," Wolf instructed.

How was she supposed to prevent that?

Fastening her gaze on Nate's face, she squeezed hard. His eyes were closed, and his breathing was ragged—then, subtly, his breathing changed. He gyrated his hips, seeking a little more pressure. She immediately released her grip.

"Good girl," Wolf approved.

Wolf's last spank forced Nate forward.

"Nicely taken," Wolf said. He set about releasing the buckles that fastened Nate to the cross.

"Can I finish him off?" She wasn't exactly sure who she was asking. Nate? Or was Wolf still in charge?

"Nate?" Wolf said.

"Somebody," he said. "Please."

Poor man sounded exhausted and frustrated. Again, she looked at Wolf. When he nodded, she knelt in front of Nate and took him in her mouth.

"I'm going to last maybe thirty seconds." Nate buried his hands in her hair, holding her steady while he pounded into her.

When he came, she swallowed each drop of his salty essence.

Nate groaned, fingers digging into her with quiet desperation. Several seconds later, voice hoarse, he said, "You're good at that."

"I liked it."

"How are you doing, Fagan?" Wolf contemplated her.

Suddenly on sensory overload, Kayla pressed the back of

her hand to her mouth. She was deep in the middle of a sex scene with two gorgeous hunks who had no trouble expressing their most erotic desires. She was unsteady, not sure what she wanted, what she didn't want.

"Are you ready for your turn?"

CHAPTER SIX

HAWKEYE

His dick hard, Stone watched her. Fagan was rubbing the back of her neck. Then, aware of his gaze, she stopped, as if afraid of betraying too much emotion. "I... Uhm... I—we—need to talk first."

"Of course." He'd have been a little concerned if she plunged ahead without due consideration. Hawkeye recruits were resourceful and smart. They weren't afraid of danger, but it was prudent to gather information before rushing in to an unfamiliar situation.

As much as he'd been watching Davidson, he'd also had his eye on Fagan. She was nervous but intrigued. She wanted to experiment but was afraid it might be too much.

Plenty of people liked their relationships with a side of spanking or spiced with a few ropes or handcuffs. He'd blazed past that years ago. For him, BDSM was a lifestyle choice, not an occasional treat, like dessert after dinner. The men and women he was involved with needed to understand this was an essential part of who he was.

"I'll meet you both upstairs." She fled.

He took care of Nate, helping him to the bench, offering him a towel. Stone looked his sub over. "You okay?"

The raw honesty in Davidson's eyes walloped Stone. "I've missed this, boss. Missed you."

Much as he wanted to, Stone couldn't admit he had also. He placed his hand on the top of Davidson's head.

"We frightened Kayla." Nate wiped sweat from his torso then dropped the towel.

"I think she's scared of her own reactions and the fact she wants to try it."

"She has the hots for you."

Stone arched an eyebrow.

"Not that she wants you to spank her, fuck her, and send her back to her bed alone. She wants more."

"Are we talking about the same Fagan?"

Davidson scoffed. "For someone who prizes observation, there's a lot you don't notice."

"She's a professional."

"And a woman." Davidson stood.

Stone took a step back as his sub brushed past.

Not looking at him, Davidson spoke again. "Women want to be loved and held." He stepped into his jeans.

"And you?"

His expressive eyes clouded with regret, with resolve. "I know it's not being offered."

"Then why are you here?"

Pretending to be interested in his zipper, Davidson glanced down.

"Davidson?"

"Look." Nate dragged a hand through his hair. "I said I got over being a fool for you." He drew a shaky breath. "That doesn't mean I got over *you*. You're a damn good Dominant. I get off hard when I'm with you."

Emotion pulsed between them, a live, dangerous thing.

"And I'm not stupid. I like scening with you, so I had a little talk with myself. I moved on with my life. But if things work out that we can hookup, then I'm up for it."

His eyes were wide, earnest, making Stone think about a future together. Ruthlessly, he shoved the dangerous thought aside.

Davidson shrugged into his shirt. "You can spank my ass anytime. You can even fuck me or ask me to suck you off. I'll take what I can get, and I promise you I'll keep my stupid fantasies locked away."

The man's admission shot pain and guilt through Stone. Uncomfortable with the unwanted emotions, he shoved them aside. "And playing with Fagan? We've never added a third."

"It changes the dynamics." He shrugged. "I'm cool with that. I want her to say yes to us. Who knows? Maybe she and I can continue to play when you vanish like you always do."

Stone curled his hand into a fist. Fagan and Davidson scening without him? Forming a bond that left him out?

Davidson picked up the water bottle and twisted off the cap. "What about you?"

"Me?"

"Are you lonely? It's a big place."

Stone lifted a shoulder. "I don't get out here much."

"Yeah. You only take time off when you're forced to." Davidson drained the bottle, then crushed it. "Seems a shame. If I were you, I'd be here a lot. And I'd love to have someone in my kitchen making a mess. I'd enjoy drinking coffee on the porch, and I'd be turned on by the fact that I had a lover around. But hey, that's just me." On his way out the door, he dropped the bottle in the trash.

Not knowing how to respond, Stone watched him go.

He hadn't spent much time evaluating his life. He went to

work. Ate. Crashed wherever there was an available bed. When he woke up, he repeated the process.

Part of him had regretted letting Davidson walk away last year. But they'd both had important missions, and neither had been willing to compromise. Davidson had left because Stone wouldn't ask him to stay. Stone readjusted the thin strip of leather holding his hair back. As for him, the idea of opening his heart was too damn big of a risk. He'd done it once, and the destroyed home, possessions, and finances that Brenna had left behind had been so painful that he'd never forgotten it.

If he were being honest, though, he'd admit the last year had been the longest, the emptiest of his life.

He wiped down the playroom so it would be ready for the next session, then he turned off the light and headed upstairs.

Stone took a left turn to the Batcave. A check of his surveillance equipment showed that all was quiet. *For now.* His teammates were right. Michael Huffman was an ugly sonofabitch with massive resources.

The night it had gone down, Huffman murdered a Hawkeye agent. If the man hadn't missed a prearranged check-in, the gruesome deaths of Lisa and Elliott Mulgrew might never have been prosecuted.

As it was, because Stone had driven over to check on his operative, he'd arrived while Huffman and his hired gun were still onsite.

Elliott's lifeless body was tied to a chair, and obviously he'd been forced to watch as Huffman raped and brutalized his wife.

Forensics experts believed that Elliott had been shot in the head in front of Lisa before she, too, had been murdered, execution style.

Stone blinked away the memory.

His lovers were in the great room, and suddenly he no longer wanted to be alone.

He shoved back from the desk, then determinedly closed the office door behind him.

Davidson sat on the leather couch, his legs stretched toward the fire he'd obviously built. Fagan was sitting on a rug in some sort of bizarre yoga pose, staring at the flames.

The weather had relented. Rain and wind no longer shook the house, leaving the atmosphere peaceful.

Davidson's words replayed in his mind. What would happen if Stone didn't keep others at a distance? If he had someone to come home to at the end of an assignment? If he could share the burden brought on by the job?

His porch had never been used, and he rarely hiked to the top of a mountain. He did, indeed, have a spot of paradise. What if it was a home instead of a fortress?

The unaccustomed, unwelcome thoughts made him restless. Instead of chasing them in circles, he compartmentalized, shifting his thoughts to what was immediately in front of him. "Does it help?" he asked Fagan. "The yoga?"

"Most of the time."

"Most of the time?" Davidson glanced at Fagan.

"Until now, I hadn't had many experiences that breathing and stretching couldn't help."

"Told you we freaked her out," Davidson said.

She unfolded her legs. For a second, it reminded Stone of a butterfly unfurling its wings.

He took a seat in the oversize leather chair. They'd left the wingback chair vacant for him. "You needed to talk, Fagan? Are you ready?"

"Yeah. About that..." She stood in a lithe movement that captivated him, made him aware of her femininity.

Men and women were built different, and he was a

connoisseur of both. He pressed his palms together and waited.

"I want to play."

"Go on."

She paced. Then, with her back to a wall, she admitted, "I'm intrigued, but I'm not sure I want to experience the same type of intensity that you two seem to enjoy."

"We've played together for a long time," Davidson said.

She looked at him. "You have?"

"Years," Stone said.

"Years," Davidson confirmed. "And he built me up to this. You wouldn't be expected to behave the way I have. He can be gentle. Well, not exactly gentle, but patient."

"Was that supposed to make me feel better?"

Davidson grinned.

"I'm not into causing undue pain," Stone said. "And I have no interest in spanking someone who doesn't want to be spanked. Everything here is safe, sane, and consensual."

"Sane?" she asked.

"Depends on your definition of sane, I suppose." He smiled. "Does Davidson over there look any worse for the wear?"

She studied him, then shook her head.

"And you played earlier. Anything too edgy about that for you?"

"It was..." She seemed to struggle for the right word. "Indescribable."

"Are *you* any worse for the wear?"

"No." She folded her arms across her chest. "I'm still horny."

Her soft-spoken admission made his cock hard all over again.

"I just...don't want anything extreme."

"You want to stay in control while you're out of control."

"Sounds ridiculous when you put it that way." She laughed, a nervous little sound.

"We'll talk it out as long as you want. And we never have to scene at all."

She nodded.

"Like Davidson, you'll have a safe word. And a slow word. We can go at your pace."

"Your safe word will stop any activity," Davidson said. "You can always say no. Your Dominant, Stone, will honor that. You get to set boundaries and negotiate terms." He moved to the edge of the couch. "Think back. When I ate your cunt…"

She blinked. Stone was enjoying this interplay between the two. Davidson knew he was a sub, had accepted it, was comfortable with it, liked it. Fagan would find out soon enough. He was glad to be the one to initiate her.

"Stone was watching your every reaction. Exploring your comfort zone is okay. But freaking out isn't. He would have stopped. When he was squeezing my balls, he was methodical, and he never stopped thinking about me, looking at me. It's fucking thrilling stuff, Kayla, all that attention. Your pleasure is the only thing that matters."

Entertaining as hell, this.

"My pleasure is the only thing that matters?" Clearly, she was confused, and a little intrigued, if the glint in her green eyes was anything to judge by.

"Who got off downstairs?" Davidson asked.

"You did," she replied.

"And look at him. Poor, unfortunate Stone is still sporting a hard-on."

Did he have to be so fucking cheery about it? "Thanks for pointing that out."

"Make no mistake," Davidson continued, "if you have any

desire to submit or learn about submission, Stone is the Dom you want."

"Davidson's right." Stone leaned forward. "We'll go slow. I'll check in with you a lot. By watching you, I'll know when you're at your limit, even if you don't realize it. You'll never be taken anywhere you don't want to go, or any place I deem unsafe."

"I..."

He couldn't help himself.

Desire for this woman with her intense green eyes and untamed auburn hair drove him to distraction.

Standing, he crossed to Fagan and closed his hands around her shoulders. He helped her up until she stood facing him, her head tipped back to meet his gaze.

Then he captured her head and kissed her long, hard, deep. Nothing punishing, nothing dominant, just gentle reassurance.

She tasted of wine, spicy and rich. And then, moments later...of surrender.

His cock pressed against his zipper, insistently, demandingly. Did she recognize her power?

Fagan swayed toward him, taking the role of the aggressor. Her tongue plunged deep into his mouth. And he was suddenly commiserating with how desperate Davidson had been to orgasm.

Eventually, she pulled away. "Oh. Hmm. Well. Wow."

"Just for the record," he said, holding her close, one hand just above her rear, the other between her shoulder blades, "I want to have sex with you. Whether or not that happens is completely your call."

"Even if...?"

"Even if I never spank your delectable ass."

"Even if...?"

"Even if you don't want to submit."

"Right now, I want to be in charge."

She wanted...? This was different, and a hell of a turn-on. He controlled her with her hair, tipping her head so she looked him in the eye. "Lead on."

After feathering her fingers into his hair, she wiggled against him. She wasn't a short woman, but she had to stand on her tiptoes to drag him closer. Willingly, he went.

This time, she kissed him, pushing against him, grinding her breasts into his chest as he put his hand on her ass to press her against his erection.

"Hey!"

Stone was aware of Davidson, but hell, he'd had his fun.

"I don't leave you guys out."

Fagan abruptly ended their kiss.

When Stone got his hands on Davidson, the man would be volunteering for sentry duty since he wouldn't be able to sit on his ass anyway.

She glanced at Davidson. "Wolf needs some attention."

"So do I," Davidson said.

"You've had plenty." She still hadn't released her hold, and Stone was grateful. "And I want a cock to play with."

Hell. The woman knew exactly how to ask for what she wanted.

"Whose?" Davidson asked.

She looked back and forth between them. "Hmm..."

Stone clenched his jaw.

"Both."

Davidson's grin was triumphant. "Told you she'd make a great third."

Stone didn't point out that he hadn't used exactly those words.

"Where do you want us, honey?"

Honey? Davidson was calling her *honey*? Why the hell had Stone left the gags in the basement?

"I want Wolf on the bottom so I can straddle him."

That got his interest. "Have we gone through enough formalities that you can get naked now?" Stone asked politely.

She scowled. Maybe he hadn't been as polite as he'd thought. He should get points for trying, though. He hadn't tossed her on the couch and taken her hard, like he wanted.

"Your bed," she dictated.

"Mine?"

"I just changed the sheets on mine," she said. "And since Davidson doesn't get to spend the night—"

"Hey!"

"He doesn't have a bed. Isn't that what you said, Wolf?" Her voice dripped sugar.

Collaborators in crime. Maybe he should make both of them sleep outside. But he wasn't capable of that. He wanted them too damn bad to even make the threat. "My bed," he agreed.

His little wannabe Domme led the way to his room. Her butt wiggled as she walked. She was denim and cotton and everything nice. Not a dominating bone in her lithe body. But he figured she'd coldcock him if he laughed at her.

She sat on the edge of the bed and patted the place next to her. "Nate, come here. And you"—she pointed at Stone—"strip."

What the hell had he gotten into?

Stone had no problems being naked. In fact, he preferred not to wear clothes. But having two lustful subs hungrily watching every move... "This is a little disconcerting."

She laughed gleefully.

"I want to see your ass first. Turn your back to us."

He raised a brow but did as she instructed. Stone removed his socks and shoes, then dropped his jeans, and he was wearing nothing beneath.

"Oh, my God. You have the sexiest butt ever."

"Glad you approve."

"Do you have an impressive cock? Or am I going to have to pretend it's big enough to satisfy me?"

Bloodthirsty little wench.

"Turn around," she said.

He did.

His cock, totally hard and demanding release, jutted in front of him.

"Come a little closer. And put your hands behind your head."

He'd do what she said, for now. But the payback would be sweet.

She closed her right hand around his cock and stroked him hard a couple of times. "Not bad."

"I'm glad I please you."

"You will." She all but purred. Then she cupped his balls.

He swallowed hard.

Right about now, he was regretting telling her how to successfully squeeze a man's nuts, creating exquisite agony but no damage.

He glared when Davidson laughed.

Fagan pulled down a bit on Stone's sac, getting his testicles exactly where she wanted them.

"Easy." But his cock swelled in her hand.

"And then I can take them both in my palm, right?"

"Your hands are smaller than mine." His breathing became shallower. He knew what he was doing when he handled another man's testicles. She was an amateur. He'd talked of trust, though, and how it was a two-way street. He couldn't very well tell her to take her hands off his jewels. "That...ohhh..."

"You can take a little more," she said. "Unless you want to safe word."

"I'll take more."

"Like you're squeezing a rubber ball," Davidson coached.

Her motions very controlled, she exerted more pressure. "Does that hurt?"

He gasped, and a bead of sweat trickled down his nape. But he kept his hands behind his head.

"Just a tiny bit more," she said.

He was going to ejaculate all over her hand.

"Much as I want you to come," she said, "I'd rather you fuck me."

"Slowly," Davidson said. "Unless you want him on his knees—in that case, tug on him and then let him go."

Half a dozen threats jumped into Stone's mind. But since his nuts were caught in a viselike grip by a beginner, he kept his mouth shut.

"It is about trust. All of it." Her gaze on him, she released him.

It'd been years since he allowed anyone to handle him like that. He didn't hate it, but he didn't intend to do it again anytime soon. "If it's all the same to you, we can experiment with your trust from now on."

"I like having that kind of power over you."

He brought his hands down and hauled her up off the bed. "You have two choices, Ms. Fagan. You can strip in under seven seconds. Or Davidson can strip you."

She looked at Davidson. "I liked being in charge while it lasted."

Davidson sighed. "Never does with the boss. Get used to it."

"I guess, since you've wasted those seven seconds, that Davidson will be stripping you."

"Uh, I'll get undressed."

"It wasn't a question." Stone was implacable.

"I…" She looked up at him.

Stone was done messing around. It was time to put things back in their natural order. She blinked several times, but he was implacable. "Your eyes are beautiful." Like moss on a sun-drenched boulder. "Batting them might have a greater impact on some other Dominant." Looking at Davidson, Stone said, "Get naked. Then take off Fagan's clothes."

Within seconds, Davidson had followed orders.

Stone released Fagan and took her place on the mattress. "Begin with her shirt. I want to enjoy the show."

With speed so slow it appeared reverent, Davidson unbuttoned her shirt. Stone liked the interplay between the two subs, the focus they had on each other.

Fagan shrugged the material from her shoulders, then gave it to Davidson, who draped it on the mattress.

"Continue."

Davidson moved behind her to unhook the bra. Then he let it, too, flutter to the bed.

"Now," Stone instructed, "let me see your breasts, Fagan."

Her head bowed, she faced him.

"Stunning." They were smallish but firm, with pouty nipples. He wanted to be inside her. "Make your nipples harder."

Using her thumbs and forefingers, she squeezed her nipples, then tugged them outward.

Christ. This wasn't one of his more brilliant ideas. His body was demanding release, not a sweet striptease. "Nice." Fuck. His voice was rough, and he wanted to show more control.

Davidson grinned. The man knew the effect Fagan was having on Stone. Not just any woman would do. He'd been with women almost as attractive, many of them much more submissive. But no other woman had literally had him by the balls. "Now the jeans."

Davidson unfastened the button at her waist before lowering her zipper.

Stone wanted more of *her*. "Turn around," he said. "Like you, I want to see your ass."

"You've already seen it!"

"Do you want me to repeat my order?"

"I wouldn't if I were you." Davidson shrugged and added, "But go ahead, if you want to live dangerously."

"I wanted to be in charge," she said.

"You were."

She turned around, facing Davidson, giving Stone a perfect view of her curvy derriere.

As Davidson worked to shove her jeans downs, she shimmied and went up on her toes. She was exploiting her power, and he should have anticipated that. Because of her little dance, it took Davidson forever to get her undressed.

She kicked off her shoes, then bent to slowly work at the last part, giving him a face full of her rear.

Enough was enough.

He grabbed her around the waist. He stood and simultaneously lifted her from the floor.

"Yikes!"

Helpfully, Davidson pulled off her jeans the rest of the way. Then Stone turned and dumped her on the bed. She tried to squirm away, but he pinned her hands above her head, securing them in one of his. He jerked off her panties.

"Careful with those," she protested.

"Too late." He tossed the scraps on the floor. "Now, where were we?" He lowered his hand so he could stroke between her legs. "You're wet." So damn perfect.

"A little."

More than a little. After teasing her for another couple of seconds, he slid a finger inside her. She moaned and parted her legs, arching her hips, asking for his cock. "You wanted me to be underneath you, right?"

"Y-yes." She seemed a bit hesitant now.

In seconds, she was on top of him, but he still had her hands imprisoned. "Like this?" he asked.

"More like with me setting the pace."

"Davidson, sheath me."

The other man grabbed a condom from the bathroom. With great care, he rolled it into place. Stone hadn't been this aroused since he saw Davidson last. "Mount me. Facing away."

First, she leaned forward to gently bite his lower lip.

Damn, she was sexy.

With her back to him, she lowered herself onto his cockhead.

"Watching the two of you is making me horny."

"She'll have to suck you," Stone said, lifting his pelvis even as she moved a bit lower. "Because I'm holding her hands."

"But then I won't be in control."

With a growl, Stone replied, "You never were."

Davidson knelt in front of her and placed one hand on her shoulder. He curled the other behind her skull to hold her head steady.

"Now give me your hands, Fagan."

She crossed her wrists at the small of her back, and Stone seized them. In this position, she was helpless.

Davidson exerted some pressure on her head, and Stone took advantage of it to sink in deeper. She moved, simulating the sex act, and he stretched her even wider.

"Wolf!"

Whatever protest she might have uttered was choked off by Davidson filling her mouth.

The two men set the pace. Stone released her wrists to

slide his hands beneath her buttocks. He lifted her, and Davidson pushed her head down.

He'd never been more turned on. Sexy Ms. Fagan rode his shaft. His male submissive's cock filled her mouth.

"I'm going to come, boss," Nate said.

"You may." He nodded at Davidson. "Be sure to swallow every drop, Fagan."

Her reply was muffled.

With a guttural moan Davidson climaxed, and he held her captive while she obediently did as she was told.

Stone showed no mercy in fucking her.

Her pussy clenched around him. After Davidson collapsed on the bed next to them, her moans became wildly abandoned.

Stone's orgasm gnawed at him, but he practiced internal muscle control, holding off a bit longer...longer...

"Wolf!"

"Come," he instructed.

She thrashed wildly, her vaginal muscles squeezing him, and screamed his name as she came.

Then, only then, did he ejaculate.

Satisfying... Very satisfying.

The trio ended up in a tangled heap on the bed. Sometime, maybe an hour later, she said, "Wolf?"

"Hmm?"

"I'll take that spanking now."

CHAPTER SEVEN

HAWKEYE

"You're sure?"

"Yes."

Nate turned on a small lamp.

Kayla studied the scowl buried between Wolf's eyebrows. It had been easier to decide she wanted a spanking when she didn't have to look at the sculptured planes of his face. "Err, I mean no." Considering a spanking was different in theory than actually exposing your bare parts to a Dominant.

Wolf laughed. "Yes or no, Fagan?"

She'd always been a decisive person. Once she made a choice, she followed through. Until now. "I... If we don't do it now, I think I'll chicken out." He'd been stroking her hair, but the moment she started speaking, he'd stopped. She was trapped between the two men, with their legs on top of hers, and she loved the feeling of being smaller, safer. She and Wolf shared an oversize pillow, and she angled a bit to look at him better.

"No pressure," Wolf said quietly. "Don't do this for me, or because you think it's what I want. I won't be disappointed if I never spank you."

"I want to do it," she said. "For me." She rolled onto her side to stroke her fingers down the center of Wolf's chest. He just stayed there, not taking charge. But from experience, she knew that would last, oh, twenty seconds or so.

Even though she was scared to go over his knee, frightened to be affixed helplessly to the Saint Andrew's cross, she wanted to experience everything. He was due to testify soon. They might never all be together again.

Even if she hated it, she'd have more regrets for not trying it.

Kayla captured his jaw and leaned in to give him a quick kiss. He took the opportunity to give her bottom a quick spank. Her eyes widened.

"Get dressed," Wolf said. "Both of you meet me in the great room."

He climbed from the bed, pulled on his jeans and a T-shirt, and left the room.

She sat up, not bothering to drag the sheet with her. "I'm confused."

"About?"

"Why he just left. I'm already naked. I figured we could just get on with it."

"It's about the symbolism," Nate explained. "Since this is your first spanking, he wants to be sure you know exactly what you're doing."

Impulsively, she gave him a quick kiss.

"You shouldn't have done that," he cautioned. "Now I know what I'm missing."

"I'll just have to give you more then."

"Promises, promises."

"You'll be there with me?"

"Where else will I go? As you pointed out, it's not like I have a bed."

"Or a helicopter to get you back out."

"Guess I'll have to throw myself on someone's mercy."

She cleaned herself up in the bathroom, then re-dressed. Nate was already waiting for her.

Nerves swamped her when she reached the great room. Wolf was in his wingback chair once again. The teasing man she'd stroked and kissed was gone. An implacable Dominant was in his place.

"Not too late to change your mind," Nate whispered in her ear.

But it was and had been since she entered the room and her gaze collided with Wolf's. His eyes were intense, their depths fathomless like a storm-tossed ocean. And she wanted to see them darken.

He'd said he wouldn't be disappointed if she chickened out, but she would.

"We'll start with over the knee."

"Start with?" Her voice didn't come out strong and determined.

"We can work up to the cross later. Have you thought about a safe word?" he asked. "And what's your understanding of how it works?"

"I'll use red. And my safe word will stop the scene."

"Begging won't stop it." Wolf nodded. "Neither will the word *stop*. Or *no*. But you can use yellow to slow down."

Since she couldn't find her voice, she swallowed hard.

His palms were pressed together, and he tapped his forefingers together. "Tears and tantrums won't stop it."

"Breathe into it," Nate said. "Use your yoga."

She tamped down her nervous excitement.

Nate moved over near the fireplace, off to her side. The fire had long since died down. Now, only the soft glow from the embers remained. The room had a chill that chased up her spine.

"Like downstairs with Davidson," Wolf continued. "I'll

give you a few swats to bring the blood flow to the region. You're less likely to get bruises or welts if you get properly warmed up. We'll start with ten."

"Softy," Nate teased.

"Her ass isn't as hard as yours, Davidson." Wolf slid a quick smile in Nate's direction. The sight of their genuine affection nearly melted her.

The clock marked off the seconds, the *tock* amplified by her nerves.

"Davidson, fetch my leather gloves from the playroom."

Nate left, and it was just her and Wolf alone. "Any questions?"

"No. I trust you."

"After the first series, if you wish to continue, I'll give you twelve well-delivered spanks."

"That's how many Nate had to take." The damnable squeak was back again. "And he's a man."

"Anything less, you might walk away with a false impression. It's my intention to be easy with you, not gentle."

Nate returned.

"Strip," Wolf said.

Her hands shook. This time, she wasn't capable of being a smart-ass. She undressed, taking her time, being deliberate with her motions. With each item of clothing that she removed, something inside her shifted, putting her in a different state of mind. The symbolism Nate had spoken of made sense now.

"When I instruct you, please walk across the room. Keep your head down, your gaze submissively at the floor."

Had Nate done that?

"Then lie across my lap. You can brace your hands on the floor. Keep your ass high, in striking position. After most spanks, you will be permitted a couple of seconds to compose yourself and get back into position. Stalling will increase the number of spanks."

When had her feet become leaden?

"All spanks will be delivered on your thighs, on your buttocks, or directly on your pussy, if you don't keep your legs together."

She gasped.

"You'll like it," Nate assured her.

She turned in his direction.

"So I'm told," he added.

"Thanks," she said.

"On no occasion will I hit you with my hand on your lower back or higher." Wolf kept his words even, explanatory, with no emotion. She truly had the sense that she could walk away at any time, that he'd take her to bed and have hot sex with her.

"Is your pussy wet?"

She licked her lower lip.

"Check," he said.

Surprising her, she was slick. With the fear that was winding its way through her, she expected to be dry.

"Now lick your fingers."

Feeling scandalously naughty, she did.

"Come to me."

Kayla took three steps toward him, then paused to recover her determination. Once her breath was steady, she continued the last few steps. Somewhat awkwardly, she maneuvered herself into position.

Wolf Stone overwhelmed all of her senses. The position across his hard, unyielding legs kept her off balance, and his denim jeans scratched her skin.

Her heart roared, drowning sound and clouding her thoughts.

He jostled her, and it was a fight to keep her legs closed,

which meant her pussy was going to be exposed to his view —and his punishment. Despite all that, there wasn't any place she'd rather be.

"You've got a gorgeous ass," he said. "Be a good girl and show me your pussy."

That wasn't so hard. It was more difficult keeping her legs together.

"So very sweet," he said, fingering her.

Her clit was a swollen nub. Unbelievably, even after their great sex, she wanted more. She wiggled, wordlessly begging him to bring her to orgasm.

Then he pulled back. Right away, his bare hand landed on her butt, straight across the middle, horizontally bisecting her cheeks. Stunned, she gasped. *This is a warm-up?*

He pressed one hand to the small of her back to hold her steady.

She thought she'd been ready for the first spank, but she wasn't.

Remembering his instructions, she prepared for his next spank. A few seconds later, it landed just below the first, and the force made her lift her head. "I can't." But that wasn't her safe word.

"Back into position."

When she was ready, he delivered another, lower and harder. "Wolf!"

He shocked her with the fourth, landing it above the first. After that, he gave her a short breather. It took a few moments to ready herself again.

The fifth scorched her labia. She screamed.

Wolf's final warm-up swats were delivered quickly, with no break between them, on either side of her butt cheeks.

"Damn you!"

"Good girl," he said.

She panted. It was over?

"Davidson, my gloves. Tell me how you're doing, Fagan."

She tried to get up, to move, but he forced her back down.

"Your cheeks are a lovely red." Nate's words went to her head, making her dizzy.

Kayla struggled to take a full breath. "I'm... Don't know what to say."

"Are you turned on?" Wolf asked.

Utterly. "Yes."

"You took those like a champ."

"Even with all my carrying on?"

"I expected it."

Somehow that made it worse. He shouldn't have expected she'd respond like that. It made her all the more determined to take the real ones with more stoicism. She thought of Nate and his quiet moans and the way his penis got harder as the tawsing progressed. He obviously hadn't been thinking of the pain.

Wolf put on the gloves and vigorously rubbed her upper thighs and buttocks. It hurt, but she forced herself to keep breathing and to keep her mouth shut instead of protesting.

She yelped when he passed a gloved hand across her already swollen labia.

"Ready for the next set?" He waited silently.

She nodded.

"I can't hear you."

"Yes."

"What is your safe word?" He rubbed her clit with the leather.

She squirmed. But like Nate earlier, she was getting more and more aroused. The leather, the pressure, her own dampness... "Red."

He tugged off his gloves and dropped them on the floor.

Before she could draw another full breath, he spanked her, his bare hand catching her already tormented skin. She moaned and wiggled. He barely gave her a second to compose herself before the next landed right below her right cheek. Then he gave her no time at all to sort out the dizzying feelings. The third, fourth, and fifth came together instantly. Tears sprang to her eyes.

"Stop thinking and struggling." Nate's voice was soothing, a sharp contrast to the way her body burned. "Keep your body relaxed. Absorb it and enjoy it."

Since she'd seen him do exactly that, she knew it was possible. But she found it almost impossible.

"You're almost halfway there." Wolf trailed his hand across her skin, changing her experience entirely.

She willed her muscles to go limp. His tenderness was a striking contrast to the burn of the spanks, confusing her neural responses. Pleasurable sensations she'd never experienced fired off inside her.

His next swat landed between her thighs.

This time, she sighed instead of tightening her buttocks.

"Much better." His praise seeped through her.

Nate's devotion now made sense, along with the risks he'd taken to return to Wolf.

"Count down the last ones, from six to one." He vigorously rubbed her behind again, and she stopped thinking.

"Six!" she managed when he landed one smartly on her right cheek. "Five!" she cried out when he placed one on the other side.

The next had a searing intensity, and she gulped for oxygen. "Four," she whispered.

Sweat slickened her back.

She forced in a deep breath, and she realized that, even though he'd made the spanks harder and sharper, she was able to handle it better.

He landed one between her legs. "Three." She shuddered. "Please..."

"Please?" he asked. "Do you need a safe word? Need me to slow down?

"No." *God.* She wanted to come. How was that possible? But she needed him to finger her clit and let her climax.

When she said nothing else, he gave her the most devastating spank yet. Her pussy clenched. Hunger clawed at her. She shook her head to clear it. Nothing existed except her arousal, the scent sharp and tangy on the air.

"What's the count?" he prompted.

"Three…?" She couldn't see anything past her own desire. He mastered her totally, completely. And her tears weren't from pain—they were from surrender.

"You're on two."

His voice was cool, calm, composed, controlled, and she reached for it. He gave her another, which left only one more.

Being naughty, very naughty, she dug her toes into the floor to readjust herself. She turned her feet inward a little, knowing it would part her thighs a bit more.

He read her wordless invitation and blazed the final slap.

She screamed.

She didn't count a number, wasn't capable of it. "I need to orgasm," she told him. "Please… Please…" She was babbling, but she'd never been this desperate before. "Please."

Hardly aware of what was happening, she was in his arms, then deposited in his chair. He knelt in front of her and put her legs over his shoulder. He inserted two fingers deep inside her, then pulled back.

"Wolf!" Then he tenderly licked her, sucking her clit into his mouth. "Bite," she begged.

He did.

She screamed as the orgasm crashed into her. She jerked convulsively and thrashed, calling out his name again and again and she rode the climax. He drew it out, gently nibbling, applying pressure, sucking, licking.

She shuddered tremendously, and when she finally opened her eyes, he was still on his knees, still between her legs.

"Well, Fagan, your first spanking is in the books. And you've set yourself up for another by orgasming without permission."

"SHE'S ASLEEP," NATE SAID WHEN HE RETURNED TO THE GREAT room. And Stone. The man who was the world to Nate. "I put her in your bed. I figured if she woke up, she'd appreciate having you in there with her."

Stone nodded, staring into the barren hearth.

Nate took a seat on the leather couch. Stone scrimped on nothing. This stuff was plush, comfortable. An exquisite handwoven blanket lay across the arm of the couch for cool evenings. Pottery decorated the mantel—one piece was a horsehair pot and another was etched. Everything in this room fit the location and its owner. He stretched out his legs toward the nonexistent fire.

"Been thinking," Stone said. "About what you said."

"Yeah?"

"This place is too big for one person."

The admission stunned Nate, giving him hope, which might be the most dangerous emotion of all. "Loneliness sucks."

Stone didn't respond. No surprise there. "Fagan's got a spankable ass."

Nate grinned. "Like mine?"

"Yours is like cowhide."

"So you have to work a little harder."

"No one has a hand hard enough to spank you successfully."

"Good thing there are other implements of torture."

"All of which I'm going to use on you."

His pulse became erratic. What this man did to him —always had.

"She's got a lot to learn if she wants to play."

Waiting, Nate remained silent. Stone was a man of few words, but he never said anything he didn't mean.

"If she wants to play with us," Stone clarified.

Nate expelled a breath. "You're not planning to kick my sorry butt to the curb?"

Stone regarded him. Tension crawled over the air like a supercharged storm. "You deserve a beating for that comment."

He hated how much he needed Stone's reassurance.

"Do you mind?"

"Kayla joining us permanently, rather than just for the moment?" When Stone nodded, Nate went on. "Not at all. Just want to remind you, though, that there isn't an *us*."

"There has been for three years. On and off."

"More off. And nothing in the past twelve months."

"Closer to thirteen," Stone corrected. "Are you ready to change that?"

Shock arced through Nate's stomach. Yes. He wanted to change that. He'd wanted to change it since the beginning. Yet emotional pain reminded him that Stone's definition of a relationship was a hell of a lot different than his own. "What if I do?"

Stone steepled his hands together and regarded him over the top. "You didn't want that last time."

"The hell I didn't." Nate surged to his feet. "I didn't want the scraps you were offering. That's different."

"Scraps?" Stone scowled. "You're calling what I offered you *scraps?*"

"Give me another word. Your idea of the perfect relationship meant that I'd be available when you wanted, at your convenience, and you could decide, on the spur of the moment, that you wanted me here."

"That's not how I put it."

"No," Nate conceded. "But that's all you were offering."

"I wanted you to share my house when we were both between assignments. I wanted you to come home to me. That's a relationship."

"Bullshit," Nate countered. "You won't open yourself up. You won't admit you want or need anyone. You're so freaking scared of being hurt again, you'd rather be alone. That's scraps."

Stone sat there.

Nate paced. "Is that what you're offering now? The same damn thing as last time?" He fought off the urge to punch something. "A relationship is when two people who are in love share everything. The good and the bad stuff. They make plans for the future. They spend holidays together. They let each other know they're alive and safe." He stopped pacing and fixed Stone with a level stare. "They don't turn down help. And they sure as hell don't shut their partner out."

"Well."

"We both know you were not offering that. If you had, I wouldn't have had to find out from Hawkeye that you'd been injured."

"You were working."

"*Fuck you.* Fucking fuck you, Stone!" He dragged a hand through his hair. "Twenty years from now, you'll still be in that chair, nursing a drink and wondering what the hell happened to your life."

"Davidson—"

"I'm not done. For the record, now that I'm here, I am not leaving you until this court case is over, even if that hurts your fragile ego. I love you, even if you're too pigheaded to accept that or return it."

Stone slumped. "I—"

"Had no idea?" Nate finished for him. "Of course not. You're so damn busy avoiding love, avoiding commitment, that you wouldn't even see the possibility. Well, there it is. I am here because I want to be here. I'm going to squeeze every fucking moment of joy from the experience."

Stone looked up. Pain feathered around his eyes in tiny lines. The man had a heart in there. "When the court case is done, then I'll go back to *work*. This time is on my terms, not yours. While I'm here, I sure as hell don't mind being your sub, because that's what I want. And adding Kayla as a third is a real turn-on."

"Now are you done?"

"I…" Nate raked a hand through his hair. "Yeah."

"Come here." There was a plea wrapped around Stone's command. "I want to kiss you."

If he'd said anything else, in any other tone, Nate might have refused. But the emotion chipped away his resistance.

Nate crossed the room. Stone stood and wrapped his arm around Nate with a tenderness Nate hadn't known possible.

This kiss wasn't about punishment, and it lacked their usual passionate aggression. It was about healing and a desperate promise to do better.

He looped his hands around Stone's neck and leaned in, simultaneously surrendering and asking for more.

Stone cradled Nate's head, holding him still.

His Dominant's tongue tasted of promise and the future. His skin smelled of the untamed power of a Rocky Mountain winter. When Nate was on a mission, the scent would find him, carried by the breeze. It tantalized him, kept him awake, his cock hard and his body wanting.

When Stone's fingers found his fly, Nate helped. He undressed quickly, surrendering when Stone said, "I want you over the arm of the couch."

Nate was prepared to be taken with force. In fact, his insides churned, ready for the possession.

Instead, Stone left the room for a minute, then returned with his fingers slick with lube.

Reaching back, Nate parted his cheeks for his lover's possession. Stone worked his forefinger in, lingered, then eased it out slowly, drawing out the foreplay. Everything about this exchange was unexpected, tripping his senses. "Stone!"

Stone paid no attention to Nate's protests as he slid a second finger inside that tight channel.

Nate forced himself to keep breathing, but his body was becoming slick with sweat, and he was desperate for sex.

When Stone inserted a third finger, spreading them, fucking him, Nate couldn't help himself. He pumped his hips in time to Stone's thrusts, and his own erection rubbed against the smooth leather of the couch. "Take me."

Deliberately, Stone sought, and found, Nate's prostate, then masterfully massaged it. Precum slickened the tip of Nate's cock. "I'm going to—"

"Not yet," Stone said, stopping his movements.

Nate pushed out a shuddering breath.

He fought to steady his heartbeat and control his reactions.

"Ready for more?" Stone asked a minute or so later. He'd leaned over Nate's body, pressing him deeper into the couch's arm, his breath warm on Nate's skin, his voice both commanding and seductive.

"I'm not sure I can take it."

Stone laughed. "You can."

He comprehended the mechanics of the whole thing. When Stone massaged his prostate, a deep, rocketing orgasm was triggered in Nate. One plus one always equaled two. What Nate always forgot when they were apart was the emotional reaction he had to Stone. His feelings for the man made the physical so much more intense. He could fight battles anywhere in the world, but when Stone took him, Nate's brain ceased to function.

Stone slipped his fingers from Nate's channel, leaving Nate wide and hungry—and unfulfilled. He could have orgasmed in seconds, but the scene would progress at Stone's pace, not his own. It was part of the thrill, all of the frustration.

Stone gripped Nate's testicles. "I want your full surrender."

He'd do anything to please the only man who'd ever dominated him.

Stone pulled down slightly on Nate's sac, keeping his balls low and away from his body.

"Make your hole available."

Nate tried to nod and couldn't. His nuts were in his Master's hand. Pain. Pleasure. He had no idea where one ended, where the other started. His cock was pulsing, demanding release. And the most overwhelming thing? He knew he'd be on his knees, nearly sobbing before Stone was finished.

Stone prolonged the agony and torture.

"On your toes, Davidson."

He was desperate, unable to think. Stone's voice was the only thing real in Nate's world.

He rose as Stone commanded, slowly so as not to alter Stone's grip on his balls and cause a slash of pain. His cock pressed harder against the leather couch as he reached back to spread his cheeks again.

"Beautiful," Stone said.

Nate was slick from the lube, and his anus was still open from its earlier preparation.

"Nice." Stone inserted a finger, then another.

Nate had already been prepared, so he accommodated them with no issue. This time, Stone was…gentle. It was so unexpected that it unraveled Nate.

"I'm going to take more from you, Davidson. Every damn thing you've got."

"Yes." He was ready. Or at least he thought he was, until Stone took a partial step forward and used that momentum to push up against his prostate again.

Instantly, Nate's cock was weepy.

He gasped when Stone squeezed his testicles a bit tighter. "Damn it!" He wanted to spill his seed all over the supple leather, but that wasn't possible until Stone decided it was.

"Shall I milk you? Or should I fuck you?"

Nate couldn't put his thoughts together.

"Both?" Stone asked.

He'd never been milked, had only a vague idea of what to expect.

"Both," Stone decided.

Expertly, Stone massaged Nate's prostate. Ejaculate leaked from him in a slow, steady stream. Despite his resolve to keep his emotions separate from their physical joining, he fell even more completely under Stone's spell.

Nate's gut was tight, and his body was all Stone's.

The flow from his cock was unlike anything he'd ever felt. Not a powerful screaming orgasm, but a slow, soulful experience. "Dear God, Stone."

Then suddenly, it changed.

Stone let go of Nate's testicles. And his cock filled Nate's ass.

He hadn't realized Stone had undressed, had no idea the man had sheathed and lubed his dick until it filled him, drove him, pounded him. "Fuck!"

"You're so damn tight, Davidson." Stone penetrated deep as he dragged Nate backward to meet his thrusts.

Even though his ejaculate had been slowly streaming out, Nate came hard, screaming as the friction of the leather and Stone's possession pushed him over the edge.

Then, and only then, did Stone come. His hard cock filled Nate's ass, and his raw, guttural moan said things he never would.

Stone bit Nate's shoulder. "You're mine, goddamn it."

Nate's knees weakened.

Right now, his life couldn't be more perfect.

"Is this a private party? Or can anyone join?"

Kayla's soft, soothing voice was as welcome as his Dominant's unyielding fucking.

"Not private," Stone said. "Get your sweet little spanked ass over here."

Nate turned his head slightly to the side to see her in one of Stone's T-shirts, the hem skirting her at midthigh. Her hair was rumpled, her features soft.

On bare, silent feet, she moved toward them. Tenderly she threaded her fingers into Nate's hair.

Her femininity—combined with Stone's alpha masculinity—completed Nate.

"I think we have enough energy left for Fagan. What do you think, Davidson?"

Perhaps Stone did. "I may need to watch."

"Take off that shirt," Stone commanded Kayla. He still hadn't released his grip on Nate.

Kayla's eyes widened, but she stopped touching Nate long enough to pull her shirt up and off.

Her pert breasts were taut, her nipples erect in the brush of cool evening air, and her labia were swollen from the spanking Stone had given her earlier.

"Have you ever masturbated in front of an audience?" Stone asked her.

"Uhm…no." She laced her fingers together.

"That chest over there?" He nodded toward the corner. "There are a couple of toys. Choose whatever you want, but be sure to grab the nipple clamps."

"Nipple clamps?" Her voice was high, a bit distrusting, and maybe a little excited.

"Nipple clamps," Stone affirmed. "But don't put them on. I want Davidson to do that for you."

Maybe he wasn't quite as tired as he thought…

CHAPTER EIGHT

HAWKEYE

Since the moment Kayla first arrived here several weeks prior, everything had been an experience. From long walks on the ranch and its rugged terrain, to lounging in the hot tub at dusk, to the first sighting of Wolf's naked, semi-aroused body, to the experience of being naked without questioning it, to having two amazingly hot men at the same time. Was she really going to masturbate, her legs spread wide as they watched?

While introducing her to things she hadn't believed possible, Wolf had pushed past limits she hadn't known existed. And his interactions with Nate stunned her. How was it possible for a man to be so commanding and compassionate at the same time? Even though he was unyielding, he never forced Nate to go somewhere he didn't want to go.

And Nate…

He was so gentle with her. The way he had carried her into Wolf's room and tucked her into bed, placing a sweet kiss on her forehead before turning off the light, had made her feel as if he'd wrapped her in a cocoon of tenderness.

From Wolf's firmness to Nate's tenderness, she was falling for them.

Conscious of Wolf watching her every move, she crossed to the chest he indicated. Could he see that her buttocks were still red from his spanking? Did it turn him on?

Kayla lifted the lid. There weren't just a couple of toys in here. There were lots of them. Dildos, some even made from glass. There were butt plugs and vibrators. And paddles and cuffs.

A shudder rippled through her as she selected a large dildo and a smallish vibrator.

Peripherally, she was aware of Wolf leaving the room to clean up, then returning with a damp cloth to do the same to his lover.

Again, a paradox.

She thought Wolf would have Nate perform the ritual, but Wolf seemed to want to do it for Nate. "Isn't that going to make him hard again?" The cloth was in his hand, and he was rubbing Nate's cock with it, in a back-and-forth stroke.

"That's the idea."

"I won't be able to walk straight for a week," Nate protested.

"Poor baby," she soothed. But she felt no sympathy. She'd have trouble sitting for at least a day. Her pussy was swollen. Every nerve ending in her body was oversensitized.

She picked up the pair of D-shaped clamps that Nate had mentioned and swallowed convulsively.

No. She had no sympathy at all for Nate...not if these things were going on her.

Nate was sitting on the floor, and Wolf stood near the fireplace, his hand extended.

"Since it's the first time you've had your tits clamped"— his raw language grabbed her attention, as she knew he meant it to—"we'll cut you a bit of slack."

Obediently she dropped the clamps into his palm. She was so aware of his body—hard angles, rough edges, and the wounds struggling to heal.

She wanted this man.

After she gave Nate the toys, Wolf cupped her breasts. "Exquisite."

Even though he'd just orgasmed, his cock was jutting in front of him. He drew her breasts together, then flicked his callused thumbs across the tips. She gasped and closed her eyes as warmth flooded her.

He laughed, a seductive, arousing sound.

Knowing she was safe, she shoved aside her nerves. She wanted to try anything he dreamed up.

He lowered his head to suck on her right breast, drawing her nipple inside and pressing it against the roof of his mouth. She moaned.

"She's going to like the clamps," Nate said.

If it was anything like this, he might be right.

Wolf lavished her left breast with the same attention. She wasn't going to need lube for the toys, as wet as she was.

When he pulled away, she sighed her frustration.

"Ready?"

She scowled. He laughed.

"Davidson, throw a couple of pillows on the coffee table. Fagan, up you go."

After Nate put the pillows in place, she climbed up on the table, aware of all their reflections in the floor-to-ceiling window dominating the west side wall. Wolf came over to adjust her body and the pillows so that her pelvis was tilted up.

He drew her toward the edge. "I want to tie your legs to the table."

Apprehension skittered through her.

"Your choice," he said.

She tamped down her fear and aimed for trust. After taking a steadying breath, she whispered, "Yes."

Within seconds, her spread legs were secured. There was no way she could draw her thighs together. Would it even be possible to orgasm like this?

Her head was on the polished wood beneath her, and her hips were elevated on the pillows. The vulnerability made her cheeks flame again.

Nate handed her the dildo she'd selected, but she said, "I think I'll use the vibrator." When the little device was in her hand, she said, "I'm not really sure how the clamps work."

"We're going to let you get aroused, get past your inhibitions. Then on my signal, Davidson will affix them, one by one. I'll tighten them as firmly as you can take it. You good?"

She nodded.

"Turn on the vibrator, Fagan."

Her fingers shook as she complied. After everything she'd already experienced, this shouldn't make her so timid, but it did.

The low hum filled the great room.

"Your pussy is swollen."

And achy.

"It's beautiful."

She used one hand to part her nether lips, not that they needed it with her legs spread so wide.

"Expose your clit," Wolf said.

She drew back the little hood to show him the swollen nub.

"Nice," Nate said.

She closed her eyes.

One of the men knelt between her legs and nudged aside the toy to lick her, from back to front. She strained forward as much as the ties would allow. Quickly, furiously, she was turned on.

As always, she wanted more. *More.*

He complied, circling her exposed clit, then pressing on it. She moaned.

Then he was gone, and he was guiding her hand toward her pussy.

She was consumed with the knowledge that they were watching her. So hot. So sexy.

Her eyes still closed, she brushed the vibrator across her clit. Her entire body tingled.

Her earlier moan became a groan.

After a few more passes, she could hardly contain her own reactions.

"Don't come," Wolf instructed.

She pulled the little device away and forced herself to breathe deep until she'd contained the orgasm.

When she was ready, she plumped her clitoris, then feathered the vibrator across it.

One of the men captured her right breast. She opened her eyes to see Nate's smiling face and irresistible blond hair.

He laved her areola with his tongue. "Keep playing with yourself."

He nibbled, sucked, bit, then captured her right breast and squeezed her nipple between his thumb and forefinger. Automatically she tensed.

"Distract yourself," Wolf instructed.

Then he was there, his hand on hers, guiding the implement. Her hips jerked reflexively.

Nate released her nipple to affix the clamp. Wolf grinned as he tightened the screw.

She gasped, but neither man relented.

Nate moved to her other breast. Wolf eased a finger into her vagina.

She was overwhelmed, done in by the tenderness, the sharp pain, and—unbelievably—the building orgasm.

Wolf continued to finger her, and she moved the vibrator, faster, *faster*—then Nate clamped her other nipple and swallowed her cry with a tender, soothing kiss.

As they cared for her, she began to relax. The sharpness of the pain receded.

And then...

Then...

An orgasm grabbed hold of her.

"Ride it," Wolf urged. He took hold of the chain that ran between the clamps and twisted it in his palm.

She thrashed.

She'd never experienced anything like this. So adored. So sexual. So *female*.

Nate deepened his beautiful kiss, and she pressed the vibrator harder against her clit. She was close, so close—just a bit more.

Wolf inserted another finger before he tugged on the chain again.

She screamed. The climax crashed against her and dragged her under. "Holy..." She couldn't find words. It took her several minutes to become aware of the world again.

When she did, she realized Wolf had released her from the bindings and was massaging her legs. Nate had a warm damp cloth pressed between her legs. She opened her eyes. "My nipples hurt like hell."

"Welcome back," Nate said with a quick grin.

"When I remove the clamps," Wolf told her, "the blood will return. It'll hurt momentarily. When we've played together for a lot longer, I might make your suffering part of the scene. But since you're a newbie..."

"Gee. Thanks. I guess."

Wolf's grin was feral.

He crouched next to her. He still favored his leg, but in his usual, stoic way, he didn't complain.

Which was more than she could say for herself when he released her right nipple. She howled.

"It's not all that bad," Nate told her.

Suddenly it wasn't. Because Wolf pressed her tender flesh with his tongue.

Her mind spun when Nate simultaneously licked her other nipple. She had two gorgeous men, one dark as night, one fair as daybreak, pleasuring her.

Their time together wouldn't last much longer, and that made her all the more determined to enjoy every single moment.

How the hell had this happened?

Stone treasured his space, his privacy. He liked waking up before dawn to grab a cup of coffee, check the monitors in his office, scan the world headlines, then working out hard before hitting a hot shower.

Instead, he was in the center of his mattress, in the middle of the night, tangled in the sheets. Fagan's fresh-as-summer hair was spread across a pillow and one of Davidson's muscular legs was pinned beneath his own.

So much for Stone's orderly, unencumbered life.

From the moment Fagan arrive with her pseudotherapy skills, his world had been turned upside down.

For weeks, he'd awakened in the middle of the night to check the house and the monitors. He'd been aware of her sleeping in the guest room, her scantily clad body sprawled invitingly across a queen-size mattress.

He was a controlled man who kept his sexual desires on a tight leash. Or they had been, until *she* showed up. Since he caught a glimpse of her cream-colored thighs, he'd masturbated twice a day.

Then Davidson had arrived, bringing with him a flood of unwelcome emotion. After they parted last year, Stone had forced himself to move on with his life. It hadn't been easy. They had a long time invested in each other. They'd met more than three years ago and hooked up dozens of times, all without making a commitment. When they slept together—fucked—they'd combusted.

Now Davidson was back, and Stone couldn't ignore his own feelings any longer. He didn't want Davidson to walk away again, which he would, if Stone wasn't able to articulate the things Davidson needed to hear.

Fuck it all.

Stone hadn't asked for this, hadn't expected it, hadn't wanted it.

He'd planned to get himself healthy, then let Hawkeye know he was ready to return to duty.

Instead, his life, and his bed, were filled with people he cared about.

What the hell was he supposed to do with all that?

Fagan sighed, and her delicate hand shifted on his thigh.

Within a fraction of a second, he had a raging hard-on. He wanted her, bad. And the image of him stuffing his cock up her tight virginal ass while Davidson fucked her sweet pussy made Stone throb. He disentangled all their limbs and managed to find his way from the bed.

He strode into the bathroom and closed the door.

Stone grabbed a bottle of lube and squeezed a dollop onto his cock, then tightened his hand around his dick and stroked. He started slowly, letting the intensity build. Everything was about control, even this.

He thought about his subs, about giving them pleasure, about how their reactions gave him pleasure. He thought of the way Davidson responded so perfectly to every command,

and he thought of the joys of initiating Fagan, experiencing her sexual awakening.

He pumped his cock.

Seconds later, he groaned, then came—hard.

Maybe being alone wasn't all he'd tried to convince himself.

Relieved—at least temporarily—he cleaned up. Davidson and Fagan were still sleeping, so he pulled on a pair of workout shorts and headed for the kitchen to turn on the coffeemaker.

Minutes later, holding a cup of strong black Sumatran brew, he headed for his office—or as Davidson called it, the Batcave.

Stone checked his monitors, called up an activity report.

Still calm.

He listened to his messages. Surprise of surprise, the trial was going well, and he would likely be called to testify sometime tomorrow.

Fuck.

He wished he had more time.

Much as he'd like to make the plans and arrangements and be done with it, he had to respect his teammates, his lovers, and include them in his decisions. He scowled. This relationship stuff was complicated. It would have been easier if Hawkeye had allowed Stone to deal with his own issues. But Hawkeye liked to meddle even more than Davidson did.

As soon as the trial was over, Davidson and Fagan would be assigned to new missions.

That thought didn't settle well in Stone's gut.

Restless, he stood and ran his hand through his hair. Then, with a tight nod, he decided to keep the information to himself for a few hours. Maybe that way he could sort through his conflicting thoughts.

When he returned to the kitchen, Fagan was already

there, her hair sleep tousled, one of his T-shirts skimming her thighs, too far beneath her buttocks for his taste. She stood looking out the window, her back to him, her feet bare.

As if sensing his presence, she did a slow pivot toward him. Her smile brightened his cloudy world.

"How's everything in the Batcave?" She took a drink from the mug of coffee she held. "I woke up when you left the bedroom. I thought you might want some privacy, so I stayed here instead of barging into your office and jumping your bones like I really wanted to."

He refilled his own cup.

"Thought I'd push your chair away from the desk and straddle you. Give you a deep kiss, then rub myself on you until your cock got hard enough to slip into my pussy."

He put down the cup before the coffee sloshed out.

She was blushing, much like she had yesterday. He found that oddly appealing. A very female reaction, even though she was an agent with one of the world's premiere protection agencies. She was a woman who knew what she wanted, knew how to get what she wanted, wasn't afraid to ask for it, and yet her face still betrayed her slight embarrassment about it all. "And I got out of bed," he said, "because I couldn't stop thinking about you holding your buttocks apart while I fuck your ass."

"Oh?"

"I was thinking about Davidson filling your pussy at the same time."

She returned her cup to the counter.

"Any lingering soreness from last night?'

"My rear is a little tender." She tucked a loose strand of hair behind her ear. "Nothing bad."

"Turn around. Bend over and show me."

Slowly, she did, easing herself over until she grasped her ankles.

"No bruising," he observed. "One small welt. Damn, Fagan, you've got one hot ass. Takes a spanking well."

When she stood and faced him again, she was smiling.

He dragged a chair away from the kitchen table and sat. "Straddle me." His words were invitation and command.

If he hadn't been observing her so closely, he might have missed the way her tongue nervously played with her lower lip. But she didn't hesitate.

Bolder than he might have expected, she tugged off the T-shirt as she walked toward him. Her responsive nipples were pebbled beautifully, begging to be teased and clamped.

Her pussy was still swollen from yesterday's session. Her cunt would look gorgeous with metal clamps tugging down on it. The image made his cock stir. "Show me what you would have done in the office."

She climbed into his lap, dug her fingers into his hair, loosening the thin strip of leather, then pulled back his head and kissed him sensually.

She tasted of cream with the bite of coffee. Beneath was the sweetness of her surrender.

As she deepened the kiss, she leaned into him, then eased back, rubbing her naked crotch against him. The material of his shorts had to abrade her sensitized skin, but her moan sure as hell wasn't one of protest.

He itched to lift her and slide her onto his dick, but he waited, letting her play out her fantasy.

In the distance, the shower ran, and Davidson hummed an off-key ditty. If he was still draining the hot water tank he finished with Fagan, Stone figured they would join him.

Fagan fumbled with his shorts. Her breaths were shorter and further between as she sought, and found, his length.

"We need a condom," he told her.

"Are you clean?" she asked. "I mean, like STDs."

"I am."

"So am I." She nipped his unshaven chin. "And I'm on the pill."

He smelled her arousal, the scent sharp and primeval. It fired the Dominant in him. She was his. And he'd have her.

She sensed the change too.

Still, his innate caution urged him toward taking care of her. "Condom. There's a box in the great room, in the drawer of the side table." He lifted his hips, shifting her off his lap.

She nodded. While she was gone, he removed his shorts.

"Let me," she said when she returned. He nodded and studied her as she rolled the protection into place. Finally, she straddled him again and took him in hand to guide his cockhead toward her entrance.

There was something amazingly sexy about fucking a woman, filling her soft pussy, feeling it conform around him. When he angled her so that he'd find her G-spot, she leaned against him for support.

Unable to let her set the pace any longer, he cupped her ass, digging his fingers firmly into her sexy flesh. He took over, guiding her actions, moving her up and down his shaft, filling her, making his cock slick with her juices.

"I'm ready to come," she told him.

Good girl. Already accustomed to offering that power to him.

"Wolf?" It was a question and plea.

"Yeah." He nipped her earlobe. "Come for me."

She writhed as she took his entire length in a single stroke. Crying out, she shuddered, her pussy clenching, driving his orgasm.

Moments later, she collapsed on him, her arms fastened around his neck as the last of his ejaculate pulsed from him.

"Not a bad way to start the morning." Her voice held a husky note that could have him hard again within a couple of minutes.

He stroked back her hair to trace the side of her neck. The idea of not having her or Davidson here was already unthinkable. "Davidson is probably still in the shower," he said.

"I bet he can't reach all the places on his back."

Stone grinned. "I'm sure you're right." He stood. After getting rid of the condom, he picked her up.

She squealed and hung on tighter, wrapping her legs around his waist. "What about you leg?"

"I can manage your weight." As he walked down the hallway toward the master bedroom, she nuzzled his neck.

In the bathroom, steam frosted the mirror. Above the shower noise, Stone called out, "Room for two more in there?"

"Thought I would shrivel into a prune before you got here."

He opened the shower door and let Fagan slide down his body. Davidson's cock was hard, his balls heavy and thick.

"There's nothing shriveled about that," Fagan said.

Davidson grinned.

"May I?" she asked, reaching for a bar of soap. She curled her hand around the shaft, and Davidson backed into one of the walls, using it for support.

For the time being, Stone was content to watch the pair play with each other.

He hadn't imagined things could be any sexier than they had been with Davidson. But he was wrong. Unbelievably wrong.

After Fagan sank to her knees, she rinsed the lather from Davidson and then took him into her mouth. Stone's cock stirred. Watching his lovers play together was damn erotic.

Even though she was servicing Davidson, Fagan looked up at Stone. Water dripped from her naked body, and her hair was slicked back and darkened. He was quite sure he'd never seen anything, or anyone, so beautiful.

He learned he wasn't much of a casual observer.

On his own knees behind Fagan, Stone teased her pussy and stroked her clit, making her move and jerk, intensifying the oral experience for Davidson, the lucky bastard.

Right this moment, his life was pretty damn close to perfect.

CHAPTER NINE

HAWKEYE

Battling to restrain his fury, Nate shoved open the door to the Batcave. "When the fuck were you going to tell us?"

Stone sat at his desk, back to the door, studying a computer monitor.

Earlier, Nate had cooked a gigantic breakfast, knowing they all needed sustenance to rebuild their energy following the previous night's activities. After the dishes were cleared, they sat at the table together, discussing world events and making plans for the day.

After Stone's admission that the house was too big for one person, Nate had dared hope that things were different. But Stone wasn't willing to change. And Nate was still as goddamn gullible as he'd always been.

Stone slowly turned his chair in Nate's direction. "I learned before breakfast."

"Which means you had, oh…two and a half hours to say something."

"I wasn't going to keep you out, Davidson."

"You already have."

"Look—"

"Shut up, Stone." Nate took two steps inside Stone's sacred sanctuary. "You can screw me into next week, but I have a mission to do. And you won't stand in the way of that." He curved his right hand into a fist. He'd been pissed at Stone plenty of times, but this fury consumed him. "Were you planning to sneak out of bed tomorrow morning and head down I-70 alone? Or truss me and Kayla up like Thanksgiving turkeys and strap us to the Saint Andrew's cross while you handled things?"

"It's not like that."

"Then how is it?" He folded his arms across his chest.

Stone stood.

Despite his Dominant's size, Davidson refused to yield his ground.

"I intended to call a meeting later." Stone's voice was dangerously low.

"Call this insubordination." Propelled by years of anguish, Nate rocked forward and landed a solid punch on Stone's jaw before striding from the room.

The satisfaction didn't fade.

Nate had no regrets, except for the obvious one...wasted emotional energy on a man incapable of opening himself up, even when his life may depend on it.

Propelled by anger and hurt, Nate jogged down the stairs to find Kayla lifting weights in Stone's gym. "We got a call."

She nodded, replacing the dumbbells on the rack. She toweled off as she followed him.

"Grab your computer. Hawkeye has sent us email. We'll use the kitchen as our command center."

"Where's Wolf?"

"Busy." He snapped the word.

Somewhere above them, a door slammed. If Stone attempted to leave, Nate would flatten the vehicle's tires.

"Would it have anything to do with your knuckles?"

"It might."

She opened her mouth as if to say something else, then closed it again.

Within two minutes, Nate was back in the kitchen with Kayla, and the computer was going through its start-up sequence.

"What do we know?" she asked, all business. It was hard to believe only a couple of hours ago she'd been in front of him in the shower, his hand fisted in her hair as she took his cock deep in her mouth.

"Stone's testifying tomorrow."

"Sooner than we expected."

"Huffman will be expecting us to move Stone under cover of night or tomorrow morning."

She nodded.

"I recommend we go right away. Hawkeye has offered a helicopter. From there, we'll transport Stone to a safe house."

"Agreed." She logged in to her computer to access the Hawkeye Security documents while he coordinated with Inamorata at Hawkeye.

"Tomorrow, we will motorcade in," Nate said. "Police have offered motorcycles and squad cars."

Nate brought over a chair and studied her computer. Hawkeye had provided maps and information about the courthouse as well as blueprints of the safe house.

"You want to talk about it?" Kayla asked.

"Nothing to say. Stone knew the schedule this morning and said nothing."

"He didn't tell you? Didn't tell *us*?" Her mouth slackened. "Who the hell does that?"

Nate remained silent. There was no ground he hadn't mentally covered.

"After everything…" Shock resonated through her words.

"Yeah," Nate confirmed. "After everything."

"So much for teamwork. I thought…" She shook her head, and her unfinished words hung in the air.

She had finished printing off blueprints when Stone joined them, leashed energy making his body taut. Damn if he didn't look good, despite the traces of red on his face.

Damn if Nate still didn't want him.

Damn. Damn. *Damn.*

"What the hell's going on here?"

"You've got sixty minutes to pack," Nate said. "Chopper's on standby."

Stone coldly arched a brow. "I'm in command."

"No, boss, you're not." Nate stood. "Take it up with Hawkeye if you have a problem. As of now, I have a protection order that covers you for the next forty-eight hours. Get used to it. If you refuse, Hawkeye will turn you over to local authorities for protective custody."

"Davidson—"

"Bring your suit."

Kayla closed the top of her laptop with a decisive *snap.*

Stone scowled.

Nate exited the kitchen. He wanted to be on his knees, his head on the ground, ass offered sacrificially for Stone's dominating penetration. That was how things should be, which made Stone's behavior all the more infuriating.

From a distance, he heard Stone ask Kayla what the plan was. Nate didn't care if she told him everything, but one thing was certain: Nate would not allow Stone to be in charge. He mattered far too much for that. And not only to Hawkeye. Despite everything, Nate would still give his life for his Dom.

An hour later, they all met in the kitchen. Guns and ammo were checked. Tactical gear in their duffel bags was double-checked.

Right on time, a four-wheel-drive that looked more like a tank than a sport-utility vehicle braked to a stop behind the house. "Kayla, you're first. Stone, you're behind her."

"This is pissing me off," Stone said.

Plenty had pissed Nate off. "Get over it."

A driver and Cole Stewart, a Hawkeye operative of the highest caliber, emerged from the vehicle. The driver opened the back door.

Nate scanned their surroundings. "Ready?"

Kayla nodded, and she headed for the door.

"You know," Stone said, leaning in so close that no one but Nate could hear, "I'm going to have your balls in a vise so tight you're going to beg for mercy."

His guts tightened, and his cock stirred at the severe promise and threat. As always, he wanted his balls in Stone's grip. He wanted to moan as the man applied exactly the right pressure to make his orgasm rocket through his body. Instead of replying, he kept his professionalism around him like body armor. "Let's move. Sir."

With a tight nod, Stone followed Kayla.

After securing the door, Nate brought up the rear.

The driver closed the back door. Nate and the operative climbed back in, and they headed down the three-and-a-half-mile dirt road toward the gate.

A guard swung the gate open so neither the driver nor Cole Stewart needed to get out.

"Is all this really necessary?" Stone asked.

Nate's patience snapped. He was tired of being second-guessed. "If you were protecting a witness who could put away Huffman, what would you do?"

Stone said nothing. There was only one answer. When a witness was this important, Hawkeye assigned a large detail.

The driver headed for a remote spot to meet the bird.

Inside, they belted in and secured their headsets.

Within hours, the three of them were locked in the safe house on a remote piece of land southeast of Denver.

Concentrating on his job, Nate explored every inch of the three-story home, beginning with the basement. It was nicely finished with a workout area and a place to play ping-pong. He climbed to the main level. The kitchen had a small table, and the refrigerator was fully stocked. The dining room table had eight chairs around it. There was a study that served as a command center with the latest surveillance equipment and access to the security panel. A living room contained the largest television he'd ever seen, and the bathroom held a full-size washer and dryer.

He grabbed his duffel from the foyer and headed upstairs. There were four bedrooms, each with its own attached bathroom.

Stone had claimed the one closest to the stairs, and he'd shut himself inside. Nate wasn't surprised. Kayla had taken a room near Stone's, while Nate opted for the one at the end of the hallway. After dumping his bag on the bed, he looked out the window to verify a guard was patrolling the backyard.

Everything satisfactory, he returned to the main level. As he passed Stone's room, the deep, resonant sounds of his voice reverberated. Nate paused to listen. Didn't take him long to figure out Stone was talking to attorneys about his upcoming testimony.

Nate continued down the stairs, checked the monitors, then returned to the kitchen to pace.

Tension hung thick and urgent, unsettling.

A few minutes later, Kayla joined him, sat at the table, and shuffled a deck of cards. She laid them out for solitaire and began to play.

Nate crossed to the window and eased the open blinds aside. He longed for the ruggedness of Cold Creek Ranch, wanted things to be the way they were before Hawkeye telephoned this morning.

"He's a hard man to love."

"Yeah." He dropped the blinds.

"Anyone with a pair of eyes can see how he looks at you."

He faced her.

"He's as torn up as you are, Nate."

When he said nothing, she turned over another card, placed the six of clubs on the seven of diamonds. "If he wasn't, he would never have taken your punch without retaliation." She put down the pack of cards. "You would have deserved it. We both know it."

"Kayla, I appreciate—"

"You're both like wounded animals. Maybe Wolf isn't capable of changing. Maybe he is. I know one thing for sure. If he is capable of changing, it will be because he loves you."

And that was the real trouble. Stone might care about him. But he didn't have the need-to-have-you love that consumed Nate.

"Don't underestimate him or how difficult this is for him."

"Kayla…"

With a small smile that eased his tension, she stood, crossed the room, rose on her tiptoes, and kissed him, leaning into him, distracting him.

"Nice scene."

At the sound of Stone's voice, Nate froze. Kayla was much more relaxed. With her hands still around his neck, she looked at Stone. "You're always welcome to be part of this. Of us."

"Do we have any coffee?"

Fuck.

Nate disentangled Kayla's arms and headed for the basement. He didn't remember whether or not the workout area had a punching bag. He sure as hell hoped so.

"What the hell is wrong with you?" Kayla demanded when Nate had left. Tension lay like a cannonball in her stomach. Just yesterday things had been perfect. Even though the mission was nearing an end, it didn't mean Wolf could be an ass. "I'm tempted to knock you out flat, myself."

"Want to try?" He took two steps closer to her.

Damn it, a ray of sun highlighted his face, revealing stress lines next to his blue eyes. She'd been right earlier. In his own way, he was as wounded as Nate.

"I asked you a question."

Instead of responding, she crossed to the coffeemaker. "I see through your bluff and bluster. Unlike Nate." She scooped grounds into a filter, then added water and set the machine to brew. "I know you really don't want coffee. Since you've been behaving like an ass, I'll make damn sure you drink it." She turned back toward him and rested her rear against the cabinets. "I don't know who did the number on your emotions, but it wasn't him. And he doesn't deserve your scorn or your disrespect. Quit punishing him for mistakes others made."

"You're treading into dangerous waters, Fagan."

"So?"

"So?" Satisfyingly, his mouth was open wide with shock.

She smiled. At this point, she had nothing left to lose, and she was going to take a swing of her own, metaphorically, if not physically. "It doesn't matter what you think. Hawkeye hired me to do this job, so you can't fire me. Nate can replace me, but he won't."

Wolf clenched his jaw, and she pressed on. "After you

testify tomorrow, we'll probably never see each other again. If you turn in a negative report about me, maybe Hawkeye will believe you, and I'll have to find another job. I've got plenty of vacation accrued, so I'll pout in Mexico on a warm beach while I drink margaritas and decide on my next step. But you won't turn in a negative report."

"Don't try me."

"You're a lot of things, including an asshole…"

"You mentioned that," he said drily.

"But you're not a petty dictator. You'll tell Hawkeye my service was exceptional, because it was." She smiled cheerfully. "But the reason you'll write a glowing report about me is because I'm one of the few individuals on the face of the planet who'll tell it to you straight. You're behaving—"

"Like an ass. Yeah. Got it. Thanks." He loosened the strip of leather holding his hair back. Then he readjusted it. There was nervousness in his gesture, a confirmation of the emotion she believed he was capable of.

"You're scared of what you feel for Nate, and maybe for me too. You're in love with him, and you're halfway there with me."

"You really—"

"I see the way you look at Nate, especially when you don't think anyone is watching you." In the background, the coffeemaker gurgled. "If you didn't care, this animosity, this push and pull, wouldn't seethe between you. He's devoted to you because he's in love with you, even though you don't deserve him."

When the coffeemaker spit out its last few drops, she poured him a cup of the wicked-strong brew and handed it to him. She poked him in the chest, making him struggle to keep the liquid from sloshing over the rim. "Last night, you two were having an intense discussion. I heard enough to know that you've shut him out before. No one can make decisions for you. But you've screwed up long enough. Unless you want to lose Nate forever, you need to fix this." She checked the clock. "I'm going for a run before dark."

"That's it? You're going for a run? You drop a bomb like that. Tell me you think I screwed up with Davidson and that you believe I'm halfway in love with you—"

"Three-quarters by now."

"You're out of line."

"Not the first time." She ignored the little jump her insides made at his pseudothreat. "Later." Kayla headed for the front door, despite the fact she despised running, especially in Colorado, where there was something like seventeen percent less oxygen in the air than there was at sea level.

He looked good with a bruise on his jaw. She'd forgotten to tell him that.

CHAPTER TEN

HAWKEYE

Stone never apologized. So when he made the attempt, he didn't do it well.

But Fagan was right. He'd handled things badly with Davidson. Stone took another long drink of the vile stuff she'd brewed, then dumped the rest of the cup's contents down the drain. After all, he wasn't the masochist.

He took a breath. Then he untied and retied the strip of leather at his nape before heading for the workout area.

For a few minutes, he stood in the entryway, he propped his shoulder against the doorjamb. Davidson was close to leaving Stone forever, and he didn't know how he would survive it.

Driven, relentless Davidson threw punches at the red bag hanging from the ceiling. His lean body was damp from the physical exertion, and he heaved a deep sigh before turning toward Stone.

"You have a wicked right cross."

"If I hadn't checked it, you'd still be on the floor."

Stone nodded and rubbed the ache in his jaw. If he hadn't

deserved it, he'd have taken out Davidson before the fist landed.

"YOU NEED SOMETHING?" DAVIDSON'S BLUE EYES OFTEN danced with devilment. At other times, they probed relentlessly. But now, there was nothing but wariness.

Stone had to acknowledge the damage he'd done to their relationship. He pushed away from the doorjamb. "I was wrong."

"Which time?"

He winced. "Most specifically, today. Earlier. You'd brought it up before. Trust. I should have mentioned, before breakfast, that I knew when I'd have to testify."

Davidson grabbed a towel and draped it around his neck.

Stone hated the emotional wall between them. Before dawn, he'd woken in bed, the other man's limbs tangled with his. And now he wasn't sure they'd ever get the intimacy back. "I came to apologize."

"Stick it. You don't mean it. But we deserve answers. Why'd you keep us out? You'd flay us for the same infraction, and with justifiable cause."

"Honestly?"

Nate dragged the towel across his brow. "Yeah."

"I didn't want the morning to end."

"What?"

"I knew the minute we got the news, things would change."

"Even from you, that's the biggest crock of bullshit I've ever heard."

Shoving aside his instinctive annoyance at being called a liar, he shrugged. "There it is, Davidson. On the table. Do with it what you want. Wasn't about me keeping you and Fagan out of the loop. That was never possible. Hawkeye knew what was going on. Either he or Inamorata would have contacted you. We both know it."

"Which makes your excuse all the more ridiculous."

"So what the hell other reason would I have?"

Davidson took a step forward. "You know time is up. Whatever you do next either deepens our relationship or destroys it. Maybe that's why you didn't want the morning to end." He balled his towel and threw it halfheartedly in the direction of the hamper. "If you'll excuse me."

Stone stepped aside. He caught Davidson's scent—clean sweat, musk, and something new. A hint of disillusionment. It destroyed him.

For Stone, left out, the rest of the evening sucked.

Davidson and Fagan watched television. They made their rounds, checked in with the rest of the team, were on constant alert. But they also microwaved a bag of popcorn and ignored his sorry ass.

As a man who'd commanded dozens of these operations, he couldn't fault their behavior.

As a man who'd never been protected before, he wanted to tear a strip from someone's hide. Maybe from two hides…

Pacing, simmering with impotent anger, he went to bed early, leaving the door open a crack. It was a silent invitation, and it was all he was capable of.

An hour or so later, lights were shut off and the television fell silent. Davidson and Fagan went to bed together…in the room across the hallway from Stone.

"CUT HIM SOME SLACK," KAYLA URGED. SHE WAS TRYING TO DO as she advised Nate. But being patient with someone when your heart was breaking was close to impossible.

They were in the bedroom she'd claimed, buried beneath

the covers. "I'm sure that apology was the best he could manage." She rested her head on Nate's shoulder, and he cradled her against his strong body.

She never remembered having this kind of easy intimacy with a man before, and it scared her how much she liked it.

"I'm the idiot here. Stone is Stone. He doesn't change. Won't change. And I *volunteered* for this."

He needed to vent, and she would listen. Wolf had been way out of line, but to be fair, he'd never made promises. He'd never even invited either of them into his life.

"You want to know the worst thing about all this?" Nate asked.

"Hmm?"

"If I'm alone with him in the future, there's no doubt I'll drop my pants and let him fuck me."

"Let him?"

"Beg him to."

"No judgment here. Emotions can make rational thought impossible. I don't have the history with Wolf that you do, but I feel his pull. It's compelling. Addictive." She turned toward him and spread her palm on Nate's chest. "And so are you." He had a sexy arch of hair across his chest, arrowing down toward his crotch. She toyed with one of his nipples, and he moaned.

"Woman," he warned.

She pushed away a little so she could trail kisses up the side of his throat.

"Take this off," he said, tugging on the hem of her nightshirt.

It was different without Wolf, but he was the one who'd made that choice. "After tomorrow..." She looked at him in the dim glow from the lamp. Kayla held her breath. After her husband's death, she'd avoided relationships. Now she wondered how she could go back to her ordinary world.

She'd stayed at her place in Chicago because it was in the middle of the country, with great access to airports. She had no family, a couple of close friends, and few possessions. Now, suddenly, hungrily, she wanted this.

"After Stone's testimony, we need to burn some real vacation time. You name the place."

She exhaled in relief, and the sound was thready. She didn't want to lose him. "There's this little place in the Mexico…"

"Yeah?"

"It's a cottage at a small resort. Very exclusive. Quiet."

"Near the beach?"

"On the beach."

"Margaritas?"

"Made from the finest tequila on the planet. Fresh lime. Sugar. Orange liqueur."

"I've got a passport."

"I'll make the reservation." She helped him get the shirt off over her head. Then he donned a condom. "How do you want it?"

"I haven't taken you from behind yet."

Wolf's earlier words haunted her, and an image of him filling her ass while Nate took her pussy made a ribbon of excitement dance through her. An immediate stab of disappointment followed. Now her fantasy would never come true.

While she climbed onto all fours, Nate grabbed a condom from his wallet. After sheathing himself, he licked the side of her neck. "Nate!"

"I like the way you taste."

His cockhead pressed against her, and she realized this was the first time she'd had his dick in her.

He was almost the same size as their Dominant, and as he

drove in, the angle allowed him deep, deep penetration. She gasped.

With a frown, he froze. "Are you okay?"

"Yes. Fill me."

He did.

He held her about the hips, holding her steady for his thrusts. He was such a different lover than Wolf, gentler.

She tried to twist her body backward so she could touch Nate, but he rode her so hard she was lost.

"Just enjoy," he encouraged.

Pleasure made her moan. Could Wolf hear them? A wicked part of her hoped so.

Nate wrapped one arm around her, then reached beneath her to capture one of her breasts so he could squeeze her nipple hard. Desire ricocheted through her. "Harder."

He applied more and more pressure, and she came, crying out, bucking, writhing, grinding her hips backward.

When she was spent, he adjusted her so she was upright, her back against his chest. She reached back to wrap her arm around his neck for support.

Nate held her tight as he thrust into her pussy. He ejaculated, whispering her name against her ear.

She was undone.

They collapsed together, entangled, breathing deep, and holding hands.

"Damn," he said. "Stone doesn't know what he's missing with his stubbornness."

"I really like the way you fuck me."

"Jesus, Kayla. I may never let you go."

She hoped he didn't.

An overhead fan cut through the warm late-summer air, cooling their sweat-slickened skin. He stroked her hair and kissed her forehead, making her feel cherished. "Glad I volunteered."

"I would have requested you if you hadn't."

"Really?"

"After Los Angeles," he said, referring to their last assignment where she'd neutralized a threat to a starlet he was protecting, "there's no one else I'd rather have at my back."

"There's no one else I'd rather have fucking me from behind."

"You really are naughty," he said.

"So spank me." She sat up and slipped back into her T-shirt, more from habit than because she'd gotten cold.

"Honey, you're so going to get it."

"Promises, promises."

Kayla wasn't aware of drifting off to sleep, but she came awake with a shuddering start.

The house was quiet, too quiet.

She listened intently. Beside her, Nate, slept. Wolf often prowled during the night. So perhaps she'd heard him.

Trying to orient, she looked at the clock. The digital display was blank, and the nightlight in the bathroom was out. Maybe there was a random power cut. But she couldn't leave anything to chance.

In the ambient light from the full moon, she grabbed her handgun from the nightstand then placed a fingertip across Nate's lips.

His eyes opened.

"Power's out," she whispered.

He nodded. Silently he pulled on pants. As Nate donned the night vision goggles that she handed to him from her bag, she grabbed her cell phone, covered it with the blankets to shield its telltale glow, then pressed number nine and Send to alert Hawkeye's headquarters to the potential emergency.

Without another word, she signaled that she would secure the upper level while he went downstairs. With a tight nod, he palmed his gun and brushed past her.

Silently, she pushed open Wolf's door. He sat up immediately, slamming her pulse into overdrive. *Please don't say anything.*

In the moonlight streaming through the blinds, she turned her gun, hoping he'd catch the glint of metal.

He did.

He slipped from the bed. "Good work," he whispered as he reached for jeans.

Voice equally as quiet, she filled him in. "Nate headed down."

"Hawkeye?" He grabbed his tactical gear.

"Notified. I'll clear this level." She started with Nate's room so she could get his night vision goggles. Then she methodically searched each room before descending to the main level.

When she reached the kitchen, she made out Wolf's ethereal, bathed-in-green image as he was preparing to go into the basement. She pointed up and made a circle with her forefinger to let him know the upstairs was secure.

He indicated his check of the main level was clear.

A loud noise crashed through the house. Adrenaline churned as they hurried to the basement.

She didn't see Nate.

A bullet streaked through the air, deafening her. Instinctively, she and Stone dove for cover. She had no idea who'd fired or where the shot came from.

The sudden preternatural silence made the ringing in her ears echo.

In the near distance, glass shattered. Someone coming in? Going out? Or a damn diversion?

Stone swept right. The ping-pong table had been turned on its side, and she crawled toward it. Keeping low, Nate made his way from the workout room toward her.

After finishing his sweep, Wolf joined them. "The fuck happened?"

"Tangled with someone. Taller than me. Twenty, thirty pounds more. My guess is he used that shot as cover as he was going out the window."

"Are you hurt?" Her heart rate gradually slowed to normal.

He shook his head. "Hand-to-hand. Maybe bruised knuckles."

"Let's be sure we're alone," Wolf suggested.

They divided the basement into sections, then, when they were satisfied no one was inside the house, they removed their goggles and Nate snapped on a flashlight.

Kayla extracted her phone from her back pocket to update Hawkeye. "What the hell happened?" she demanded. No one should have known about the safe house.

"Assets are securing the premises," their contact, nicknamed Lifeguard, responded. "Cole Stewart is your point person. He'll be on-site in three minutes."

"We'll need a window repaired and the power restored."

"And transportation out of here," Nate added.

She passed along his message.

The men headed upstairs, and she remained in the basement, guarding the window. The lights flicked on, and she exhaled deeply. A moment later, her phone rang.

"Premises are secured." Lifeguard's voice was cool, controlled, as it always was.

Relieved, she joined Wolf and Nate in the kitchen. Nate balled his hands, then opened them again.

"Let me see," she said.

"Nothing that hasn't happened before." He regarded Wolf. "Recently, even."

Nate's knuckles were scuffed, with a few streaks of blood. Over his protests, she grabbed a washcloth and dabbed away the damage before smoothing on some antibiotic ointment from the nearby first-aid kit.

Cole arrived less than three minutes later. Dressed all in black, the jagged scar on his handsome face a visible reminder of the dangerous work he'd done while undercover in some of the world's most tumultuous spots, he was lethal when required. Hawkeye was lucky to have recruited him.

By unspoken accord, the four of them gathered around the kitchen table.

"Update?" Nate demanded of Cole.

"We had two men outside." A pulse ticked in his forehead. "They took out one. Inamorata arranged transport for Joseph Martin to a local hospital." His voice was icy.

Haunted, Kayla wrapped her arms around her middle. She shot Wolf a glance. Great risk accompanied protection jobs. They all knew it, accepted the reality. But that never made loss easier for her.

"We don't know how many there were," Cole finished.

"At least one got away." Nate repeated the vague description he'd given them earlier.

"We'll do what we can." Cole nodded. "Car's waiting. Be ready to roll in…" He checked his phone. "Five minutes."

They were ready in four.

Wolf remained mute as they were transported to a hotel in downtown Denver. The building had recently undergone security upgrades because a head of state would be staying there later in the year.

In the underground parking garage, the driver navigated to an elevator, then parked inside the compartment. The lift, with the car and all its occupants inside, made the ponderous trip to the thirty-first floor. Inamorata—Hawkeye's right-hand woman—met them when they stepped into the luxurious suite.

She excelled at cleaning up situations, and that included

dealing with various law enforcement agencies. No matter the time of day, she never had a single hair out of place. Her mascara never smudged, and she could kick ass, even in heels. Inamorata had hired Kayla after the debacle with her husband, and Kayla was fiercely loyal to the other woman. "How's Martin?"

"In surgery." Inamorata glanced away for a brief second. "It's touch-and-go."

"*Fuck.*" Wolf sank onto a couch while Nate paced.

"We're grateful," Kayla said.

"I'll let him know." Then, back to business, Inamorata confirmed pickup for tomorrow, then strode to the car, leaving silence once the echo of her heels on the polished tile floor faded away.

Kayla rubbed her lower arms, suddenly chilled from the post-excitement letdown.

"I meant it earlier," Wolf said. "Great job, Fagan. Davidson is right to want to serve on the same team as you."

But the man they'd lost... Unwanted emotion walloped her. "If anything had happened to either one of you..."

Wolf met her gaze. She saw something there, raw and uncontrolled. He might never admit how much he loved Nate, how much he cared for her, but it was reflected in the depths of his blue eyes.

"Hell of a night," Nate said.

Wolf didn't respond, and he seemed more of an island now than he ever had been.

Suddenly, she was exhausted and needed to be alone. "I'm going to take a shower." A bath would be better, but they had to get ready to transport Wolf to the courthouse in a matter of hours. Soaking away the stress was a luxury she didn't have time for.

Wolf grabbed her wrist as she walked past him.

She blinked as he pulled her toward him and kissed her

hard and deep. She tasted the hunger he tried to keep under control.

As he ended the kiss, she placed her hand alongside his jaw. She stayed there for a moment—as long as she could without emotionally fracturing—then extracted her wrist to walk away without a backward glance.

CHAPTER ELEVEN

HAWKEYE

Despite her intention to remain detached from Wolf, awareness pulsed through Kayla.

He stood in the main area of their hotel suite, wearing a tailored suit that hugged his wide shoulders and followed the contours of his trim waist and hips. The dark charcoal color complemented his skin tone, making his blue eyes all the more electric. The crisp white shirt with the conservative blue tie at his throat added a splash of color. As always, his hair was cinched at his nape. He was devastating.

She shouldn't have allowed herself to fall for him, yet how could she have helped it?

"Morning." He glanced at her.

She tipped her head back, pretending a professional detachment she didn't feel.

"I wanted to say thank you. Protecting me hasn't been easy." He cleared his throat. "I haven't made it easy."

"Just doing my job."

Nate strode from the bedroom he'd shared with her. Since he wasn't going into the courtroom, he was dressed in a T-shirt and a windbreaker that hid the gun tucked into his waistband. Black boots, tight jeans, a leather belt, and dark sunglasses perched on top of his head slammed her hormones into overdrive.

"It's been an honor serving on your detail, Stone. After your testimony, there will be a chopper waiting."

This was it?

Nate's phone signaled a message. "That was Inamorata. Car's on its way up."

"Davidson..." Stone straightened his tie to cover the fact that his voice had cracked.

"We have a job to do, and we'll get it done."

The elevator dinged, forcing them to shove aside personal issues.

Cole was waiting for them. As they approached, he opened the vehicle's back door. After everyone was situated, their bodies a little too close, he took his seat next to the driver.

On the slow trip down he outlined the plan to get Wolf to the courthouse then back out of Denver. "Any questions?"

Wolf remained mute while Nate shook his head.

Tension arced across the air, and it wasn't the ordinary silence that accompanied pre-mission preparation. It had underpinnings of anger and hurt, emotions she couldn't afford to look at. With a sigh, she leaned forward to tap Cole's shoulder. "How's Martin?"

He glanced back to look at her. "Still in ICU. Surgery went well, and the doctors are optimistic."

With relief, she exhaled. "I'd like to go see him when this is over."

"I'm sure he'd appreciate it."

It was after rush hour, and thanks to the police escort that allowed them to blast through stop signs and traffic signals, the trip only took a few minutes. By the time the driver braked to a stop, Kayla was focused on the job ahead.

"Showtime." Cole exited the vehicle, then opened the back door.

As arranged, Kayla slid out first. Wolf followed, and Nate brought up the rear. Behind a cordoned-off area, a gaggle of press, with reporters and camera crews, went live.

As prearranged, she, Nate, and Cole formed a protective shield around Wolf then accompanied him to the courthouse entrance, where they were met by armed guards.

"Good luck, boss." Nate nodded.

"The car will be waiting when you're ready," Cole added.

Kayla went inside with Stone, and once they cleared security, they made their way to an elevator.

"Look, Fagan...Kayla—"

"Please, don't." The rawness in his voice and the fact he'd used her given name for the first time would unravel her if she let it. "I need to do my job." When they reached the courtroom, she pulled open the door and followed him inside.

At that moment Michael Huffman looked over his shoulder, found Wolf, then smiled warmly, like he was greeting a long-lost friend.

Kayla wasn't prepared for the sight of Michael Huffman. In her mind, he was evil incarnate, his dead eyes soulless. In reality, he was stunningly handsome, vibrantly alive, with the presence of a movie star. His body was toned, without an ounce of excess fat. His suit was both expensive and respectful, and his legal team was straight out of central casting. The lead attorney was male, nonthreatening, and next to him was a beautiful blonde. If the jury saw what she did, prosecutors had an uphill battle.

"He's a snake," Wolf said, as if reading her mind, "and I'm going to be the one to put him away."

Nate hated waiting.

He wanted to be inside. Even more, he burned with the need to meet Huffman in a dark alley.

To work off some of his energy, he paced. Checked his phone. Looked at his watch.

Only a minute and thirty seconds had crawled by.

It didn't matter that he and Stone were barely speaking, Nate wouldn't rest until this whole damn thing was over.

A hotdog cart vendor opened for business, and lunchtime escapees from nearby office buildings headed for restaurants and shops. Members of the press drank coffee, all while watching the exit.

He strode around the small plaza, constantly on alert, while Cole remained with the driver, ready to bring the car around.

Nate purchased a soda from the hotdog cart vendor. The night had been brutal, and residual adrenaline churned through his system.

A guy who'd been sitting on a bench stood, smoothed out his slacks, and adjusted his sunglasses. He then picked up a briefcase that had been stashed behind a nearby planter.

Fuck.

Nate dropped his drink to sprint after the guy. "Freeze! Don't let him through!"

Onlookers grabbed their cell phones to capture pictures, and reporters went live. Terrified screams rent the air.

Near the main entrance, he caught up. Nate threw himself forward, slamming them both into the ground.

The man howled in outrage.

Furious, releasing the energy and anger churning in him, Nate slammed the guy's head against the ground.

Security and uniformed officers swarmed them. Two snapped a pair of handcuffs on Nate while three more struggled with the bad guy.

"You're going to fucking die."

Nate sneered. "Then I'll see you in hell."

———————

ENERGY JUMPED THROUGH STONE.

A memory haunted him—of Lisa Mulgrew's raped and savaged body. Hawkeye had lost men because of Huffman, and another operative was fighting for his life in a hospital. How close Huffman's thugs had come last night pissed Stone off in ways nothing ever had. He couldn't bear the thought of harm coming to Fagan or Davidson.

For those reasons, he lasered in on revenge.

He and Fagan were seated in the last row. He recognized a handful of people in the room, including Inamorata.

"The prosecution calls Wolf Stone."

Fagan touched his thigh, but he didn't respond, fixating on his task. He stood, then straightened his spine before walking down the aisle.

Instead of continuing to the witness stand, he stopped at Huffman's table. Five seconds, five seconds—that was all Stone needed to make Huffman snap.

"Sir!" The bailiff took several steps toward them.

Stone placed his hands on the table and leaned toward Huffman. "Rumor has it you fuck donkeys." He sniffed deep. "Not enough for you to rape women, is it? You'll go after anything that can't refuse your pathetic advances."

Huffman blinked.

Noise swarmed around Stone—the judge's gavel, buzzing conversation, the slow, steady beat of his heart.

"Donkeys." Refusing to let the other man look away, Stone adjusted Huffman's tie. Then he yanked the man closer. "It's true, isn't it? Everyone knows it." After pushing

Huffman away, Stone wiped his hand on his slacks in mock disgust.

Huffman shoved his chair back then stood to slug Stone.

Stone grinned, big, primal. "Donkeys."

"Two million dollars," Huffman shouted, "for anyone who kills this motherfucker."

Huffman's attorneys wrestled him to his seat, and the bailiff took Stone to the marble floor.

The murderer fought off his lawyers to go after Stone again, and several officers rushed into the courtroom to subdue Huffman.

The jury had heard the death threat. Stone calmed. He couldn't bring back Lisa and Elliott Mulgrew, but there was cold pleasure in knowing Huffman would never see daylight again.

CHAPTER TWELVE

HAWKEYE

"That was Inamorata," Kayla told Nate, coming up behind him on the patio of their private and secluded cottage on the beach. She slid her hands over his shoulders, then down his chest, when he turned toward her. "The jury returned a guilty verdict." She placed a kiss on the side of his neck.

He smelled of sunshine and ocean air, and he tasted of the bite of saltwater from his earlier swim. Suddenly, she wanted to be back in bed with him, his cock pounding her the way it had earlier that morning.

They'd arrived three days prior. After their initial tension had ebbed, the lack of adrenaline had dropped them on their collective asses, and they'd slept for nearly twenty-four hours straight. Since then, they'd talked, swam, walked on the beach, had several margaritas, and had sex at least six times.

"Stone?"

"She called him with the news before notifying us." Then she answered the unasked question. "She didn't mention how he is." Didn't say if he was lonely in that house on the huge spread of land. Didn't say whether he missed them—the way they missed him.

Neither she nor Nate had spoken much of their lover. But they were hyperaware of his absence, of the hole left in their lives and in their interaction with each other. Pain grooved a deep path between Nate's eyebrows, making her hurt. "How about another swim?" Anything to make him enjoy their stay.

"Woman, you're going to exhaust me. And then I won't be able to make love for half the night."

"I bet I could solve that problem." She traced her right hand lower, seeking his cock. Instantly, he swelled in her grip. He turned and grabbed her. She squealed as he shifted their positions, pulling her over his knee.

He tugged up her oversize T-shirt and tugged aside the crotch of her bikini bottom, fingering her damp pussy.

She wiggled.

He found her clit, plumped it, then stroked it.

"Just what the hell do you two think you're doing?"

Nate froze.

She froze.

Wolf?

She had no idea he even knew where they were.

She heard the breeze through the palm trees and the thunder of her own heartbeat.

"I asked a question."

Tension oozed through her, slowing her blood and her reaction time. She struggled to maneuver enough to see him, but from her position, she could only see his jean-clad calf. Nate, the torturous ass, put a hand firmly on her back, preventing her from moving.

"I was planning to spank Kayla," Nate said.

"You were not!"

"Yes, I was." He landed a quick, hard smack on the

buttocks to shut her up. She gasped. "And then I was going to fuck her into tomorrow."

"And who gave you permission to spank my sub?" Tension, thick and awful, laced Wolf's tone.

His sub?

Maybe she'd had too many margaritas yesterday.

"Both of you, on your knees." Wolf's voice was implacable. Her stomach plummeted.

Nate sucked in a deep, desperate breath as he helped her from his lap into a standing position. As her T-shirt fell into place around her thighs, she looked at Nate. Hope and distrust warred in the depths of his eyes, and her love flared protectively.

Even though all her instincts urged her to follow Wolf's orders, she shook her head. "Not until I know—*we* know— why you're here." They deserved an answer.

"Because I was going out of my mind." Palms turned up, he took a step closer to them. He winced in pain and tried to cover it by pressing his lips together. So tough yet vulnerable. "I missed you both."

He propped his index finger beneath her chin, tipping her head back so he could capture her gaze completely. Those stress lines were still grooved next to his haunted blue eyes, more deeply than she remembered. While she and Nate had rested, Stone had obviously not. No matter how hard she'd been suffering, so had he. A wave of tenderness washed over her.

He dropped his hand to face Nate.

"I don't deserve your love." His voice broke. "But if you'll let me, I'll work my ass off for the rest of my life to earn it."

"Fuck it, Stone. That's the only thing I ever wanted."

Wolf kissed Nate with passion she'd never seen. Their Dom was holding nothing back.

When their kiss ended, Wolf captured her shoulders. He

claimed her mouth commandingly, communicating his lone-liness and relief.

"Am I welcome back?" he asked when he finally let her go.

She wanted a future with a hunger that bordered on desperation. "That's up to Nate."

"You were right all along," Wolf admitted to Nate. "The house is too big."

"That all, boss?"

The hoarse emotion in his voice strangled her heart.

"No." Wolf curled his right hand into a fist. "I need you. I..." He looked at the sky and took a breath. "I love you. I want forever. I don't know how to do that, but we'll figure it out. Together."

Nate's strong shoulders rolled forward. "Boss, take me," Nate begged.

"And you, Fagan? Will you have me?"

His raw vulnerability healed a place in her that she hadn't known was broken. "Yes. I want you to stay."

Wolf sighed, betraying how important their answers had been.

"Boss..."

"Yeah, Davidson, I will take you. As hard as I want. As hard as you deserve."

The transition to Wolf being in control was natural and restored the perfect order of their relationship. "Now, both of you, if you can trouble yourselves to follow my earlier order..."

They scrambled to obey.

"Let's get one thing straight," Wolf said as they knelt in front of him. "From here forward, spankings will be admin-istered by me, as will all other forms of discipline or chas-tisement."

"Yes, boss."

"Or directed by me." He looked at Nate. "It may please me to watch Fagan torture your balls, for example."

Wolf was a master of so many things. Even the cadence of his voice was enough to make an orgasm unfurl inside her.

"Your safe word, Davidson?"

"Red."

"And yours, Fagan?

"Also red," she said.

"Hands behind your neck," he instructed.

Her swimsuit bottom was suddenly drenched.

"Fagan, I want you naked, but do not get off your knees." He pulled a chair back from the table and watched her pull the T-shirt over her head and then struggle with her bikini bottom. She was aware of the sway of her breasts as she twisted and lifted one knee, then the other.

Finally, she was naked.

"That's beautiful. You'll be kept that way more often. And you…" He cast a gaze at Nate. "Stand and strip."

Nate did, taking his time, obviously taunting Stone, who definitely deserved it.

"Bend over the table."

She still marveled at the smoothness of Nate's responses, how quickly he complied with his Dom's orders. Despite the warm Mexican air, she shivered.

"You'll be next, Fagan," Stone said, looking at her, even as he stood and moved next to Nate. "Pay attention, because when it's your turn, we'll be seeing how much you've learned. It'll go easier on you if you're obedient."

"This time, we'll be adding an element," Stone said, cupping Nate's balls.

Nate's breath coagulated in a lump at the base of his

throat. He honestly hadn't believed Stone would come for them. After he'd left court, Kayla and Cole had hustled him to a helicopter and back to Cold Creek Ranch while Nate was tied up with the authorities. The recovered briefcase had held a plastic gun, one that would have likely gotten through the security screening.

It was later that night that he and Kayla had arrived back at the hotel suite, their stay thoughtfully paid for by Hawkeye.

They'd made love, and she'd fought back tears, telling him they'd be okay without Stone. Both of them had recognized the lie, but neither said that aloud, as if admitting it would make the world implode.

Nate had been surprised that Stone hadn't followed her. He believed they mattered to Stone, but obviously not as much as he'd hoped.

Now, he realized, he'd been wrong.

Stone cared. It had just taken losing them both to galvanize his actions.

He pulled down on Nate's testicles, centering his attention. He sucked in a breath but then forced himself to give up, give in, surrender to the scene. If he fought it, the pain would be too intense.

"Legs a bit farther apart."

He did as instructed. Everything but Stone and the sensations he evoked faded away. Gently, the sound of the surf receded. Even the picture of sweet, sexy Kayla, naked and kneeling nearby on the patio, became more distant.

"Do you need to be tied?"

The pressure on his balls intensified.

"Davidson?"

He shook his head.

"Safe word?"

"Red." It didn't matter. He'd never use it. Whatever his

Dom wanted him to experience, Nate wanted it too. Stone never lost control. Nate trusted that. This scene would unfold more intensely than any other ever had. Instinctively, he knew that. There'd been too much hurt for the scene to be typical. Stone needed to apologize in his own way. He needed to take Nate to a place he'd never been.

Nate reached across the sturdy wrought-iron table and held on to the far side. Stone manipulated Nate's balls lower in their sac. More than scaring him, the action thrilled him.

Stone pressed his thumb to that tender area between Nate's anus and scrotum. The nerve endings fired off sensations of pleasure. His cock jutted forward helplessly.

"Ready?"

He took a couple of breaths. "Yes, boss."

Instead of squeezing his balls together, Stone slapped the taut sack.

Nate jerked. His head came off the table.

Kayla's faint gasp penetrated his haze.

"Excellent," Stone said. "Not that I expected anything less."

Nate gulped the humid air.

"Maybe another five?"

Another five? For a total of six? But he knew Stone wouldn't proceed without his consent. The pain was exquisite. "Yes, boss." He schooled his thoughts and grabbed the edge of the table harder.

The next spank wasn't as shocking, but it was even more painful.

Stone waited.

Nate remained silent.

The third made his toes curl.

Stone pressed a finger to Nate's anus, driving him out of his mind.

Suddenly, Stone took away his finger and used his hand to deliver another slap on Nate's balls.

His knees weakened. He loved Stone's demands.

He was swimming in a red haze when Stone was finally done.

"Your cock looks beautiful," Stone said. "What would it take to make you come? Three strokes?"

"Being touched," he admitted. Just having a hand curled around his dick would be enough.

"Stay there," Stone told him, "in position, until you're more under control."

What? Stone had taken him to the edge and was going to leave him there, trembling until the need to ejaculate abated?

"I'm going to release your balls."

Nate took several controlled breaths as Stone let him go.

"Put your hands behind your neck," Stone told him.

He complied, meaning his whole body weight was supported on top of the table.

Then he heard Stone tell Kayla, "Now as for you..."

And her breathless response... "Yes, Sir?"

For Wolf Stone, life didn't get any better.

Of course, it had sucked pretty damn bad before it had gotten better.

After Fagan and the other members of Hawkeye left, he'd been at Cold Creek Ranch by himself. Every room he'd been in had reminded him of Davidson and Fagan.

He'd climbed on a four-wheeler for most of a day, riding the fence line, trying to exhaust himself.

He'd gone to bed and tossed and turned, unable to sleep. Fagan's feminine scent clung to one of his pillows, and the discarded clothes Davidson left behind had walloped Stone with sexual hunger.

As he stared at the ceiling, his thoughts spun back in time. Having Davidson walk out once had been hard enough. He'd be an idiot to let it happen a second time.

He had his privacy. For what?

To wake up alone? To roam on his eight hundred acres by himself? To drink coffee in front of the fireplace with no one to talk to?

He realized the pain of being alone was greater than the risk of being hurt.

What could be better, really, than two greedy subs he loved?

It had taken some fancy talking to find out where Davidson and Fagan had headed, and then some fancier talking to secure the use of Hawkeye's private jet. Stone intended to stay down here with his subs for at least a week. He wanted to make sure both of them knew how much he wanted them. "Fagan?"

To her credit, even though she looked up, she stayed in position. He'd never tell her, but he appreciated her unabashed greeting. He'd been a little hesitant when he walked through the patio door of the beach cottage. "You're going to take Davidson and me at the same time."

"Okay," she said. She licked her bottom lip a bit nervously. "One in my…"

"Cunt," he supplied. "And me in your ass."

Eyes wide, she glanced at his crotch.

"I'll prepare you." He looked at Davidson. His cock was still thick. It'd look good filling Fagan. "Meet me in the bedroom. My travel bag has lube and condoms in it."

She stood slowly. She didn't question his orders, and her movements were feminine as she grabbed his travel bag and walked into the house.

To Davidson, he said, "Come here."

He appreciated the sight of his lover as Davidson did as he was asked. He stopped bare inches from where Stone stood.

"It's good to see you, boss."

Oh yeah. Coming here had definitely been the right decision.

They found Fagan sitting on the edge of the bed, nervously rolling the tube between her palms. "We'll be patient," he told her. "Lie back."

While she did that, he took the lube from her, dropped it onto the nightstand, and shucked off his clothes. Davidson put a condom on his dick. Then he climbed on the bed and began to kiss her. Stone positioned himself between her legs and licked her cunt, sucking on her clit.

She arched and thrashed, closing in quickly on an orgasm. "She's greedy," Stone said.

"Insatiable," Davidson complained. "I'm glad you're here. I couldn't keep up."

Stone chuckled.

He flipped her over and immediately felt the tension in her body. "That'll make it worse," he said. "On your knees, forehead on the mattress, arms behind your neck again." Then he scowled. "Actually, Davidson, over here."

He issued instructions until Davidson was beneath her, his arms wrapped around her middle. While Stone lubed her, Davidson would be eating her out. Nice solution all around, except for the temptation of Davidson's erect cock in Stone's face.

"I want you to relax," he told her. "Even when it's difficult, I want you to surrender to Davidson and bear down against my fingers." When she nodded, he spread her cheeks. "Keep your ass high," he said. He squirted lube near her opening, then added more to his fingers. "While Davidson licks you, I'm going to work a finger inside you."

The idea of taking her there made his cock thicken and lengthen. He loved introducing his subs to new sensations. He still had one or two more surprises for the remainder of their vacation.

She became still and all but stopped breathing when he pressed a fingertip to her anal whorl. Davidson, to his credit, simply inserted a finger in her pussy. She mewed and moved against him, and Stone took advantage of her distraction to push past her sphincter in a single motion.

She gasped. "Ow!"

"That was perfect," he told her. "You took my finger as if you were meant for it." Before she protested more, he slid his finger all the way out, then pushed it back in.

He and Davidson found a rhythm that she liked, and while she rode both of them, he stretched her, slipping in another digit.

She started to wiggle, trying to get away. He slapped her buttock soundly. "Ugh," she protested.

But he was relentless, fingering her ass, stretching her hole wide to accommodate his girth.

Her breathlessness and frantic movements told him she was near an orgasm, so he gently lifted her, helping her ease onto Davidson's already sheathed cock.

"Damn," Davidson said. "You're tight. And I'm ready to explode."

Maybe it had been a bit unfair to deny his sub's orgasm outside. But when he did come, it would be even more powerful.

"I'm nervous," she admitted.

From his position behind her, Stone kissed her neck. Davidson pulled her down to kiss her. That angle was quite convenient for Stone. It tilted her body, exposing her ass to him completely.

After rolling a condom onto his cock, he squeezed a liberal dollop of lube into his palm and coated himself with it. She was slick on the inside, and her body was ripe for him.

He held his cock in one hand, positioning its head at her opening. "You'll want to bear down," he told her. Since she tensed up again, he fingered her, while Davidson encouraged her to ride him.

Stone sucked in a breath as he began to enter her ass. Pushing past her sphincter was almost enough to make him come. On the flight to Mexico, he'd fantasized about this moment. Reality was even better.

"I..." Whatever she was going to say was lost as Davidson captured her mouth.

"Bear down," Stone instructed, then pushed deep.

"Fuck." She arched up and cried out. "You're going to split me in two!"

"My wonderful Fagan, you're there." He soothed his fingers across her skin.

"I'm there?" She exhaled.

"Yeah." He'd claimed all of her. Stone got lost in his thoughts. She was so tight, and the feel of Davidson inside her as well... He dragged himself back under control. "The worst is over. Do you need me to pull out?"

She wiggled around.

He gritted his teeth.

"No," she said. "It hurts, but I want you both to fuck me. I want to belong to both of you."

Over her shoulder, he met Davidson's gaze.

How the hell had he nearly let stubbornness stand in the way of this? Stubbornness? More like stupidity.

She pushed back against him, as if seeking more.

Together, he and Davidson fucked her hard, both of them claiming her, and through her, each other.

"I…I need to come," she said.

When he didn't say anything, he saw her shoulders tense up, as if she fought to stave it off. "Take it," he told her. "You earned it." How the hell had he gotten so lucky? He bit her shoulder.

She screamed, the shudders of an orgasm lashing her. To Davidson, he said, "You too."

The feelings of both of them rippling with climaxes made him heady and humble. He took his own release, pulsing deep inside her ass.

Long minutes later, they lay together in a tangle on the bed. She was between them, all their bodies slick with sweat and satisfaction.

By next week, they'd both be in his home, in his bed, with him forever.

EPILOGUE

HAWKEYE

K ayla exited the helicopter on the rooftop of Hawkeye
Security's building near Denver.

Wolf and Nate stood there, arms folded. Nate wore a welcoming grin. Wolf hungrily devoured her, assessing every detail.

Her men.

Tension drained from her, and love flooded in. She'd been gone for two months, and what felt like a lifetime.

After thanking the pilot, she ran to them, dropping her bag before falling into their arms.

Mindful of other agents and the always prying eyes of security cameras, she didn't give in to the temptation to kiss them madly. "What are you doing here?"

"Taking you to a hotel," Nate answered.

"But…" She searched both of their faces.

Nate shrugged.

Even though it was after eleven p.m., procedure dictated that she had to be debriefed and then signed out for her two-week leave. She'd been prepared to spend a couple of hours taking care of her obligations before driving back home.

"You're not due back until 0800," Wolf said.

The unexpected change of plan made her pulse flutter. "How did you manage that?"

"Spousal privilege."

"Spousal…" She frowned. "But we're not—"

"We will be."

Her knees weakened. If her Dom's hands hadn't been wrapped around her shoulders, she would have pitched forward. They had talked about marriage, in abstract terms, and they'd agreed to wait a year before making any decisions. But Wolf wasn't known for his patience.

"What he's not saying is that he threatened Hawkeye." Nate grinned. "Stone has resignation letters prepared for all of us."

Wolf pulled back on her ponytail. "We're not waiting a goddamn minute to have you in our bed."

The assignment should have lasted thirty days. But the world's youngest self-made female billionaire disliked the replacement that Hawkeye had sent and she'd insisted that Kayla's contract be extended. So that had meant an additional month without her men.

"I want you out of here and out of those clothes."

"Kayla may need to eat," Nate pointed out as he led the way to the exit. "Or sleep."

"She can sleep when we're done with her."

Excitement chased away exhaustion.

Within minutes, she was in the back of Wolf's oversize SUV, snuggled up with Nate. More than once during the drive, Wolf glanced in the rearview mirror to capture her gaze.

And every time it did, she read the same thing in his eyes. *Possession.*

When they arrived at the nearby Sterling Skyline Hotel,

Wolf turned the keys over to the valet, then assisted her from the vehicle.

A bellman hurried over for her bag, but Nate insisted on carrying it, which meant they were alone in the elevator. Nate stole the first sweet kiss, making her heart swell with love. And then Wolf consumed her with the second, making her want to slide to her knees in total submission. Each man caused a different but equally powerful response in her. With every breath she took, she'd missed them.

"Fifteenth floor," a soft female voice announced over the speakers.

Wolf swept Kayla from her feet. Yelping, she put an arm around him.

Nate pressed his finger to a pad on the door, and the lock snicked open. When Sterling had built the hotel, they'd hired Hawkeye to ensure all security measures were state-of-the-art. Not only were the views of the Rocky Mountains breathtaking, but the property was now the destination of choice for visiting celebrities and dignitaries.

Her lovers had secured a suite and thoughtfully provided her favorite wine and a cheese-and-fruit platter to go with an assortment of crackers and olives.

Nate, always the practical one, insisted she eat. She had only taken two bites when Wolf stalked her.

"Keep eating."

How could she when her mouth was so dry?

"Davidson's right." He unfastened the top button of her white Oxford shirt. "You need to keep up your energy." Slowly, he dragged a knuckle across the tender skin of her chest, making her think of surrender. "You're so gorgeous." Another button yielded, then another.

Nate used a remote control to close the blinds as Wolf tugged her shirttails free of her waistband.

"I should shower." She looked up at her Dominant and found no quarter in the depths of his hard blue eyes.

"You'll need to later."

Over the six months they'd been together, Wolf hadn't been shy about taking either her or Nate, no matter the circumstances. They could have been sweat slick from hiking or fresh from bed. Once, he'd entered their fitness room where she was doing bench presses. After she racked the weights, he yanked off her sports bra and skimpy shorts and fucked her on the workout bench.

Now, Nate walked over to join them, his cock pressing against the zipper of his jeans. Gratitude for her lovers engulfed her. Between them, they met all her needs, from physical touch to a support system that was there when she returned from duty.

Wolf had turned out to be more demanding than she'd imagined, unwilling to accept a superficial relationship. The three had regular discussions about the nitty-gritty of life, and there was no hiding from each other. Until she'd been with Wolf and Nate for a couple of months, she'd had no idea how badly her former husband's betrayal had affected her and the emotionally shallow way she'd been living her life to avoid being hurt. Instead of pretending she hadn't been married to a dirty cop, she'd talked about his betrayal—at frustrating length—until their patience and lack of judgment had broken past the barriers she'd erected to keep her heart safe.

In return, Wolf had trusted them with his past, Brenna's insecurities and neediness. One day, convinced he didn't love her because he didn't return from an assignment on time, she destroyed their home, stabbing their mattress with a knife and ripping out the stuffing. She'd smashed their photographs and dishes. And she'd cut up all of his clothing.

His rigidity had made more sense, and that knowledge

granted her and Nate more patience with Wolf. Slowly, over time, their Dom was becoming more flexible. But never in the bedroom or playroom. Thank God.

Nate eased the shirt from her shoulders, then unhooked her bra. Her breasts spilled into Wolf's waiting palms, and he closed her flesh in his hands. Crying out, she swayed forward. Nate placed his hands on her waist, steadying her, like he always did. She wasn't sure how she'd managed without him in her life.

Wolf brushed his thumbs across her nipples, and the slight abrasion shot arousal straight to her pussy.

When she was working, Kayla rarely masturbated. She could survive without pleasure for thirty days, and the hunger she had when returning to her men made the sacrifice worth it. But as the last assignment stretched into two months, her insides had become a tangled knot of need.

"It's been a while." Wolf tipped his head to the side to study her.

"Yes."

He pinched her nipples, and she sank her teeth into her lower lip. Most of the time, she liked more pressure than that. But absence had made her sensitive.

"Davidson, take over."

"Happily, boss." From behind, he wrapped his arms around her.

With a nod that served as instruction to Nate, Wolf released her. Nate brought up his hands to palm her breasts.

"Squeeze her, pinch her, and don't let her know what to expect."

Nate rolled her already hard nipples between his thumbs and forefingers.

"You're driving me mad."

"I think that's Stone's intention." Nate's words were soft against her ear. Soft but not reassuring.

"I want you undressed the rest of the way." Wolf tapped her right ankle, and she lifted each foot in turn so he could remove her shoes and socks.

Nate's attention made her wild, and she was hardly aware of Wolf unbuckling her belt before getting rid of her slacks.

She stood in front of him wearing only a pair of skimpy panties.

Over the fabric, he fingered her. "You're wet, Fagan."

"Yes, Sir." Her voice was breathless, and her vision was going black. Even though he hadn't penetrated her, Kayla was ready to come undone.

Wolf continued to toy with her as he met Nate's gaze above her head. "Shall we take the edge off her, Davidson?"

Please, she wanted to beg. But Wolf had a plan. He always did. He put as much time and energy into planning a scene as he did leading a mission. His intensity gave her one more reason to love him, even if going at his pace frustrated her.

"Davidson, on the bed."

"Yes, boss."

Nate took his time releasing her breasts, and when he did, she sucked in a breath that did nothing to steady her.

Wolf took his hand from her pussy. "Take off your underwear."

Trembling, she did as he said. Despite the time they'd been together, being nude while the men were fully dressed still made her extraordinarily aware of her submission.

Nate led the way to the bedroom. The housekeeping staff had already turned down the bedding, and Nate kicked off his shoes before climbing onto the mattress.

"Straddle his face, Fagan."

Seriously? Her mouth went slack as she looked at Wolf.

"Do it."

Without hesitation, Nate offered a hand to help her into position.

Shaking, she climbed onto the bed. As she'd closed her eyes on the helicopter, she'd pictured her homecoming. They'd all be naked, fucking. They'd kiss and hug, maybe laugh. Even in her fantasies, she couldn't have imagined it would be this wonderful.

To steady herself, she took Nate's hand. His grin told her he was completely happy with Wolf's plan.

She spread her thighs and lowered herself toward him.

"That's it." Wolf's voice was rich with encouragement.

Nate's tongue found her clit, rocking lightning through her. She flattened her palm on the headboard to stop the world from spinning backward.

"Fight off the orgasm as long as you can."

"Yes…" she mumbled, closing her eyes. *Sir* was supposed to follow it, but the concentration it took to follow his order meant she couldn't finish her sentence.

"Lean forward more."

Kayla had kept a young, energetic billionaire safe for two months, yet she was unable to follow Wolf's simple direction.

He crossed to her and pulled back on her hips, tipping her into the position he wanted. Nate immediately sucked her clit into his mouth.

"Wolf!"

"Not yet, Fagan." He slid a finger into her, then used her juices to dampen the finger he pressed into her tightest hole.

Panting, she dropped her forehead to the headboard.

"This is preparing you for later." Wolf's voice was rough. From his own desire? Was he as undone by this as she was? "I'm showing you some mercy because it's been so long since you've had my cock up your ass. You might want to express your gratitude."

She murmured her thanks.

"Tell me you want another finger up there."

Frantically, she shook her head. It wasn't possible.

153

"That wasn't a question, Fagan."

An orgasm was starting to bloom, consuming her.

"Tell me."

"Yes." Tears stung her eyes. "Give me a second finger, Sir."

"That's our good girl. Now reach back to spread your butt cheeks to make it easier for me."

His instructions forced her to concentrate on something other than coming. For that, she *should* be grateful.

Nate was there for her, lifting up her shoulders for support as she reached back to do as Wolf had said.

Relentlessly he inserted a second finger, then moved back and forth, forcing her forward with each forceful thrust.

"I… *Please*, Wolf."

When he gave permission, Nate licked her harder, the two of them taking her over the edge.

With her eyes closed, she tipped back her head and cried out, coming harder than she ever remembered.

Her body went limp. She wasn't sure which man took care of her, but when she blinked the world back into focus, her head was on Nate's chest, and he was stroking her back. Wolf stood next to the bed, a thumb hooked casually through his belt loop, grinning.

"Pleased with yourself, Stone?" Nate asked.

"I will be soon." He excused himself to the bathroom.

She inhaled Nate's fresh scent, underlaid by a spicy cologne.

"It's good to have you back, Kayla."

"I'm not sure I want to be gone that long ever again."

"Stone was driving me crazy. I was about to go and fetch you myself."

A minute later, Wolf returned with a washcloth and gently bathed her.

Kayla surrendered without protest. After being on guard for so long, it was pure luxury to have someone care for her.

"Since Fagan looks as if she could sleep for a week, I'll let you undress me, Davidson."

"I thought you'd never ask, boss."

Nate pushed off the bed, and Kayla rolled onto her side to watch. She hadn't forgotten how much she loved seeing them together.

Nate tugged their Dom's belt free, then rolled it into a tight circle that he placed on the nightstand, close enough that Wolf could grab it if he chose. Then Nate drew Wolf's T-shirt up and off. Rather than fold it properly, he dropped it to the floor.

Without instruction, Nate knelt to remove Wolf's boots, then his jeans. As he lowered the zipper, he looked up. Their Dominant dug a hand into Nate's hair to imprison his head. How well she knew what Wolf's attention could do to a sub's desire to obey.

"May I remove your boxers, boss?"

"You may."

Excitement built in her, and she reached a hand between her legs to ease the sudden ache.

"I wouldn't recommend that." Wolf's cold voice contained the fury of a gunshot.

She froze. He hadn't even looked at her.

"Come here. Kneel next to Davidson, with your arms behind your neck and your knees as wide as possible."

She didn't dare complain about being tired or just having arrived home. When she was with him, he dictated the terms of the scenes. She should have asked—

"Move it, Fagan."

Throwing off her lethargy with a sigh, she got into position.

"Wider. No way am I allowing you to try for an orgasm."

"Yes, Wolf."

"I enjoy your obedience." His smile was broad and his voice deep.

Nate finished undressing Wolf, and his magnificent cock filled her vision. It was hard, throbbing, for them.

"You're going to suck it." He guided Nate's head toward his dick. Then he spared Kayla a glance. "Open your mouth and keep it that way."

She did as he instructed, even when her jaw started to ache. Watching had been one thing, but being this close made her yearn to participate. Instead, she was forgotten.

"It's going down your throat, Davidson. Don't you dare gag." He surged forward and held Nate's head steady. "Eyes on me. I want to see your tears."

As if he'd said the horrible words to her, her pussy flooded.

Proving she hadn't been forgotten, he spared her a glance and placed three fingers in her open mouth. Maybe being ignored was better.

"Suck them, Fagan."

He tasted of soap and domination, and she couldn't get enough of him.

"Keep it up." Then he looked at Nate. "How much more can you take?"

From her peripheral vision, she saw Nate lock his body in place, struggling against his needs in order to subvert them for his Master.

This scene was hotter than anything they'd shared, more strenuous because of their commitment and the number of times they'd been together. It hadn't been long since she'd considered spanking extreme.

Her breaths were frantic as she continued to suck on Stone's fingers. He spread them, owning her mouth and her reactions.

"Good work, Davidson."

Nate shuddered as he released Wolf's dick.

"You as well, Fagan." He slowly extracted his fingers from her mouth, and she gulped in a grateful breath, letting her shoulders fall forward. "No, you don't. That was preparation."

"Sir?" Dread tap-danced up her spine.

"It's your turn."

"I…" She'd deep throated him a couple of times, but her skill level was nothing compared to Nate's. Because of her training with Hawkeye, she could hold her breath underwater for a couple of minutes, but it was something she hated doing.

"Your nose against my crotch, Fagan. Get to it."

Why, oh why, had she decided to play with herself while watching Nate undress Wolf?

She licked his shaft, tasting the saltiness of precum, easing back, thinking too much, trying to prolong the inevitable.

"That's enough stalling."

Unlike Nate, she gagged while easing Stone's massive dick down her throat. She pulled back, gasping for air. With the back of her hand, she swiped stray hair back from her forehead. "Sorry, Sir."

She glanced up to see him grinning.

"Behind her, Davidson. Keep her body occupied. And Fagan, this isn't the first time you've done this. Think about pleasing me. Do what you need to do. We have as long as it takes for you to do as instructed."

Which meant they didn't get to have sex until his demands were satisfied. Resolved, she nodded.

He guided her head back to his cock. Tentatively she swirled her tongue around the head then pressed against his most sensitive spot. Her big, bad Dom groaned. The power of that gave her all the resolve she needed to suck him deep into her mouth.

157

Nate reached between her legs to stroke her clit. She jerked, and Wolf tightened his hold on her. She was swimming in a million sensations, struggling for breath, to do as instructed, and not fall into the abyss of the climax that Nate was offering.

"You're so hot, Kayla," Nate said.

"But your nose isn't touching my crotch, Fagan. Balls-deep. Do it."

Her whole being buzzed from Nate's compliment and Wolf's relentlessness. Nate pressed hard on her oversensitized nub, and she scooted away from him. Wolf took full advantage, forcing her to take the rest of his cock.

She tried to sputter and pull away, but he held her secure, even as Nate slipped two fingers into her pussy.

Tears from her struggle spilled onto her cheeks. She'd never been more overwhelmed. She wanted this to last a lifetime.

"Well done, Fagan." Wolf loosened his grip, and Nate moved away from her, leaving her limp and frustrated. "I'm proud of you. That took a lot." He helped her up and swept her into his arms.

Grinning, she curled against him. His husky appreciation renewed her, made her happy she hadn't considered using a safe word.

He carried her to the bed and glanced Nate's direction. "Get rid of your clothes, grab the lube, and get your hot ass over here."

"Yes, boss."

"You can take Fagan's pussy. I'll have her ass."

"But…" She frowned.

"Problem?" Wolf asked.

"I'm getting all the pleasure this way."

"We've missed you. We'll have a week together at the ranch before Davidson deploys."

She was greedy enough not to protest any further.

Wolf teased her pussy, bringing her to the edge before telling her to kneel on the side of the mattress so he could lube her ass. "Now add some to my dick." It wasn't an invitation.

He pumped several large dollops into her palm, and she sensually applied it, liking the sight of precum weeping from his cockhead. Early on in their newfound relationship, they'd each gone to a medical clinic for testing so they could have sex skin-to-skin. There was nothing she liked more than this kind of intimacy.

"That'll do." Wolf wrapped his hand around hers, forcing her to stop, and she turned her head to hide her grin. "I want to fill you, Fagan."

This was the way it should be. The three of them together, naked, hiding nothing, offering all.

Slowly, she lowered herself onto Nate. Then she angled forward as Wolf knelt behind her to press against her rear. Even though he'd finger-fucked her ass earlier, she wasn't prepared for the intrusion of his massive girth stretching her apart as Nate filled her pussy. "Oh…" Her breaths were shallow. She was no longer certain she could go through with this.

"You're always capable of more than you think." It was as if Wolf read her mind, and he pressed forward as he spoke.

"Fuck," Nate muttered. "This fit is tight, boss."

"Yeah." Wolf adjusted her so he could sink his cock to the hilt.

She exhaled shakily when she'd taken all of him. She was so full that she was barely aware of the thin membrane separating her lovers.

"Yeah." Wolf's word fell somewhere between approval and a curse.

Nate captured her breasts and pressed them together. That was too, too much. "Wolf…"

"You deserve it. Come for us, baby."

The climax smashed into her, pitching her forward. Wolf clamped her hips and continued thrusting.

"Damn, boss. That friction…"

"Do it," he commanded.

Impossibly, Nate's cock grew as he arched, rising higher inside her.

Another orgasm crested before the first had fully receded.

With a controlled snarl, Wolf ejaculated. She shivered as her body tried to recover from the pleasure, the stress, of taking them together.

They collapsed together, entangled. She was back where she belonged. Satisfied. Satiated.

Perfect.

"MORE COFFEE?" NATE OFFERED.

"Please." Kayla watched the nectar of the gods fill her cup, not convinced there was enough caffeine in the house to get her going.

"Boss?"

Wolf shook his head.

As she stirred cream into the dark depths, Nate placed the carafe on a hot pad.

They'd been back at Cold Creek Ranch for two days, and Wolf had wasted no time taking them to the dungeon. Because it afforded greater intimacy, he preferred to have her over his knee for a spanking, but this time he affixed her to the Saint Andrew's cross that she'd learned to love.

After he'd satiated both her and Nate, the three showered together before entering the hot tub to relax with a glass of wine as fat, fluffy snowflakes fell around them. Like she had after the mission that brought them together, Kayla had slept for almost a full day. She'd only climbed out of bed to eat a bowl of soup that Nate had prepared. Wolf had given her a massage, sending her back to sleep with a small sigh.

This morning, she'd slept until ten, and they waited to have breakfast with her.

Nate had prepared fluffy waffles with strawberries and cream to go with a gigantic pile of bacon. Surprising them all, she'd eaten the majority of the food.

Afterward, she'd offered to clear the dishes, but Nate insisted she had one more day to relax. She vowed to return the favor next time he came home from an assignment.

Wolf excused himself. "Please wait here for me."

He strode from the room.

"Is everything okay with him?" she asked Nate over the rim of her cup.

"No idea."

Wolf returned a couple of minutes later, carrying two manila folders. He slid one in front of her. "What is this?" Kayla glanced at him, nerves assailing her. "You're making me nervous, Wolf."

Without response, he offered a second to Nate. "Open them. Both of you."

She glanced at Nate. A frown was burrowed between his eyebrows. Whatever Wolf was up to, it was obviously a surprise to him too.

Uncertain what to expect, she flipped open the cover. Her eyes went wide. She knew what she was seeing—she just didn't comprehend his meaning. "This is a copy of the deed to your house."

"*Our* house," Wolf corrected. "And the land."

She shook her head. "I don't understand."

"Boss?" Nate closed his folder, then tapped his finger on it.

Wolf took a seat at the head of the table. "You think of this as my house. I'm making it clear it's our home. There are obviously some forms you need to sign, but we are all equal owners."

"But…" She blinked, flicking her gaze between the two men. "Wolf, you don't need to do this."

Wolf pushed back his chair to stand again. He paced to the window and stared out at the expansive frosted landscape.

She and Nate exchanged puzzled glances.

A moment later, he turned back to them and dragged the tieback from his hair. The betrayal of nerves from the cool, in-charge Wolf startled her.

"When you got off that helicopter at headquarters, I talked about spousal privilege. I want to marry both of you, and that's not possible legally, but there is plenty I can do to ensure we are committed to each other." He flicked a haunted, loving glance at each of them.

Her heart swelled. His struggle was obvious, and she loved him all the more for it.

"Davidson and I were talking while you were gone, Fagan. No decisions have been made because that's not the way this relationship works. But it makes sense for one of us to marry you. I mean… *Crap.* I'm fucking this up. I was trying to be romantic." He stuffed the strip of leather into his pocket. "We want you to be our wife."

Swimming in a pool of hope, confusion, nerves, and excitement, she collapsed against the back of the chair. "You want…"

"In case, you know…" Wolf shot a frantic look in Davidson's direction.

"Babies." Davidson grinned.

"Babies?" Hot breath seared out of her lungs.

"When you're ready," Wolf added. "If you're ready. If you never are, that's okay."

"We can adopt." Nate's voice was cheery. "I'm ready to be a daddy. Stay-at-home. Or we can get a nanny."

Thank God they'd waited until she'd slept to spring this on her.

"You can think about it," Nate said.

"It's time we made all of this official. I want you both to be part of my life, forever." Weak sunshine filtered through the window, playing on the almost-blue highlights in Wolf's hair.

Tears clouded her vision.

He crossed to her. "Davidson, front and center."

Nate pushed away from the table to stand next to her, in front of their Dominant.

Wolf reached into his pocket and pulled out two rings. One had a stunning diamond that flashed fire as it moved.

Nate gasped. *"Boss?"*

"Davidson, yours is titanium. Almost as hard as your ass." Wolf cracked a smile.

"Oh fuck, Stone. I didn't expect this."

"Yeah. I know. That makes it all the better. I like surprising you." He ran his knuckles down Nate's chin. "Will you accept this as a token of my love and commitment?"

"I've dreamed of this moment since the first time I saw you, boss."

Nate extended his hand, and Wolf slid the thick band onto Nate's finger. Kayla swallowed the knot of emotion that clogged her throat.

"Fuck, yes!" Nate fist-bumped the air.

They kissed, with passion, with promise, and she had to swallow the knot in her throat. When Wolf eventually drew back, Nate couldn't stop grinning, and he ran a finger across his ring as if to be sure it was real.

"And you, Kayla." Wolf turned toward her, sucking the oxygen from her lungs. He only used her given name when something mattered to him deeply. "Will you please stand?"

Nate stopped admiring his titanium band to pull back her chair and help her up.

"I love you." Wolf's confession was husky with emotion, making her heart race.

"And I fell in love with you in Los Angeles," Nate added. "Long before we were sent to protect Stone."

At the word *protect*, Wolf shot Nate a quelling glance. His smile was so big, he didn't seem to care.

Wolf refocused on her, placing his hands on either side of her face. "Your ring was designed by both of us. It's platinum, a metal almost as precious as you are to us. Will you accept it as a token of our love and commitment? We will cherish you always." He lowered himself to one knee.

The world rocking beneath her, she reached toward his shoulder, but she was shaking so hard that she lowered her arm again. She'd been in life threatening situations, and she'd never lost her composure like this.

Wolf captured her hand and held it steady, there for her like he always was. "Damn it. Say something." Apprehension, real and thick, made his voice hoarse.

Nate wore a silly grin.

"This is sudden." And so wonderfully perfect.

"You'll have plenty of time to adapt. We won't pressure you to set a wedding date—"

"Or have babies right away," Nate interrupted.

"Please say you'll accept our proposal." Wolf's voice wavered.

Kayla met his gaze. "Yes." Seeing the beauty of their future in the clear blue depths of his eyes, her tears spilled. "Yes, yes,

yes. A hundred thousand times, yes. I love you, Wolf." She looked at Nate, and his grin made her heart soar. "And you. I love you, Nate."

Wolf slid the engagement ring onto her finger. Breathless, she stared at the stunning round diamond. It was framed by two infinity knots made up of dozens of micropavé diamonds. It shimmered with a promise of the future.

"It's meant to represent our union," Nate said. "All of it woven together."

"It couldn't be more perfect. Like both of you."

Wolf stood and drew her against him and opened his arms to Nate as well. She hugged her men, kissing them both, soaring beneath their exquisite attention.

"Are you rested up?" Wolf asked, eyes darkening.

"There was a reason for the big breakfast." Nate stole another kiss, harder than ever before, expressing his emotion through physical touch.

Life couldn't be any better. Her heart raced, and heat chased through her. "What do you have in mind?"

"Getting started on those babies."

"Davidson!" Wolf's scold was immediate.

"Well, even if we don't get her pregnant, it will be fun trying." He slipped a hand between her legs.

Even though she was dressed, he aroused her immediately.

"I thought we'd begin with the Saint Andrew's cross." Wolf scooped her up and jostled her until she was against him.

Whistling, Nate led the way to the basement.

Their Dom stripped off her shirt while Nate worked her shorts over her hips.

"And when I'm done with you, we're going to fuck you."

"Spousal privilege," Nate added, leading her to the cross, her favorite place to receive Wolf's attention.

Nate tapped her thighs, in silent instruction for her to spread them wide.

With Wolf standing over them, Nate licked her, making her moan and arch toward him. "I think I may end up liking this whole marriage thing."

"We're going to be damn sure you do." Wolf selected a flogger and carried it to her. "Welcome to your home, Fagan."

She would have answered, but she was lost, surrendered to the happiness and completion they'd brought her.

Thank you for reading Come to Me. I hope you loved spending time with Wolf, Kayla, and Nathan. I've adored this trio forever, and Hawkeye and his badass alpha operatives have a very special place in my heart.

Fall in love with your next irresistible Hawkeye agent in Trust in Me, a forbidden relationship romance. Inamorata is his boss. And his assignee is the boss's little sister, and her life is in danger. Trace Romero will do anything to protect her. But who will keep the sweet and lovely Aimee safe from his searing need for her?

DISCOVER TRUST IN ME

Hold On To Me, features a dangerous, sexy cowboy who becomes a reluctant bodyguard. (And you can catch up with Kayla as well!)

Cowboy and former military operative Jacob Walker can't refuse one last mission, protecting the beautiful, fiery Elissa. But she refuses to be whisked away from her life like a terrified damsel in distress. But that's exactly what happens when she finds herself thrown over the muscular shoulder of one very inflexible, annoying, and handsome, alpha bodyguard. Once she's at his remote ranch she discovers something much more dangerous than the threat facing her—her very real attraction to her smoking-hot captor.

★★★★★ Super hot and super sexy! Love these two!!!
~Amazon Reviewer

DISCOVER HOLD ON TO ME

Turn the page for an exciting excerpt from TRUST IN ME

TRUST IN ME

CHAPTER ONE EXCERPT

Aimee adjusted her earbuds, then headed toward the front door for her late-afternoon run. It'd been a hell of a day, and she needed the stress relief. She turned the knob, then screamed. A large, gorgeous man stood on her porch, arms folded across his broad chest.

Stunned, and more scared than she would ever admit, she froze.

He moved toward her, galvanizing her into action. She took an immediate step back, then shoved against the door to slam it.

"Wait!" He placed his booted foot in the entrance, blocking her efforts. Not just a booted foot, she noted wildly —a massive one, with the black leather riding boots showing nicks and scars—from a life on the edge if her guess was correct.

Her pulse slammed into overdrive.

Crap, crap, crap.

"I'm Trace Romero," the man said, pushing back against her.

Would a potential bad guy introduce himself? Her older

sister carried a gun while Aimee was the nerd with the iPod, ponytail, and a scientific mind that rarely shut down. They were both employed by Hawkeye Security, but since Aimee worked in IT, she'd never gone through firearms or specialized tactical training programs.

"I'm from Hawkeye. Your sister sent me to stay with you for a few days."

Her breath whooshed out.

She should be relieved, but she wasn't.

Two hours prior, she'd returned from the coffee shop to find the back patio door slightly ajar. Concerned, she'd notified her sister. The fact that an agent was standing on Aimee's porch meant her sister had called out the cavalry in the form of one of their colleagues.

And she didn't want him here. Hawkeye was one of the planet's most exclusive security firms. They hired only the most qualified operatives, recruiting from the military and police, even the FBI or Secret Service.

But that didn't matter to her. She had no intention of letting an arrogant alpha male inside her home. She'd learned her lesson with know-it-all men, and she was too smart to repeat the mistake.

"Please step back, ma'am. Ms. Inamorata is expecting a report from me."

"You can tell her you were here and that I sent you away. Mission accomplished."

"I'm afraid I can't do that. If I don't answer your phone when she calls, I might as well turn in my resignation and throw myself off Pikes Peak, save her the effort of hunting down my sorry carcass."

Aimee's running shoes slipped as he threw his strong shoulder into the door. For all the success her efforts were having at keeping him out, she might as well be trying to hold back an avalanche.

Maybe she couldn't beat him when it came to physical strength, but she could batter his ego and get under his defenses. "I can't believe a big, strong man is frightened of my sister."

"Terrified, actually. Like all mortals," he confessed.

"Damn." She groaned. His ego was intact enough for him not to rise to her bait.

"You have two choices, ma'am." His deep voice was controlled and clipped. "We can do it my way." He paused for a couple of beats, then added, "Or we can do it my way."

She hated having people in her space. It was bad enough sharing the fifteen hundred square feet with her rescue parrot that rarely shut up, but having someone around who would watch her television, eat her food, discover her deepest secrets...

The brute of a man nudged her back another few inches. "It's okay to stop the badass act." But a panicky little part of her was afraid it wasn't an act at all.

"Step away from the door, Miss Inamorata." This warning wasn't as friendly as the previous one had been.

So maybe she didn't carry a gun, but she'd learned a few things from listening to her sister. If you can't go through, go around. "Okay. You win."

He stopped pushing. She counted to two. When he let down his guard, she grunted and then shoved forward with every scrap of determination she could summon.

But her pissed-off best wasn't good enough.

His foot was still firmly lodged in the entrance.

Within seconds, he filled the space.

Good God, he was big. Bigger than big.

Instinctively she took a protective step back. No matter how mad she was, she would never be able to win against this man.

He dominated the space and sucked up the air she'd been

intending to breathe. He stood well over six feet tall, and his shoulders almost filled the width of the opening.

She, who rarely got flustered, was immobilized. Agent Romero made her oh so aware of being a woman. In her shorts and tiny tank top, she felt small, vulnerable, while he was spectacular, from his angular cheekbones to his military-precise haircut and rich, deep brown eyes. His skin revealed a Spanish heritage, and it might have been a shade or two richer for having been in the sun. His strong jaw was set in an implacable line. In every way, he spelled danger.

He took her shoulders, moved her back a foot, then released her long enough to turn, slam the door, and turn the lock...all before she could even draw a protesting breath.

"My way," he reminded her.

From the other room, Eureka squawked.

"What the hell is that?"

She should probably warn him about Eureka, her blue-fronted Amazon parrot, but it would be much more fun if he found out himself. "It's my bird."

"Inside? A pet?"

"He thinks he's the boss around here."

"Anything else I need to know?"

"I'm pretty boring." She shrugged.

"Not if someone broke in."

"Maybe I left the patio door ajar myself." But that couldn't possibly be true. Because she wanted to keep Eureka safe, she was careful to keep all possible escape places closed.

"The local police said there have been no other reported break-ins, and I understand nothing was taken?"

"That's true." Her electronics were still in place. None of her jewelry was missing. Even her emergency stash of twenty-dollar bills remained untouched in her dresser drawer.

"Which means it wasn't a random thing, and you and Ms.

Inamorata know it. Want to show me around?"

"No. Not really," she said, not even trying to disarm her words with a smile.

"You can show me, or I can look myself."

His way. Or his way. "There's not much to see. My bedroom, which you're not going into, my office, which you're not going into, the kitchen, dining room, the guest bathroom, and my living room...which you're standing in. That's it."

He took another step toward her.

The scent of him seared her, like a cool Colorado breeze wrapped in the spice of night.

Reluctantly she ceded the ground. Just as fast, she regretted her action. Instead of remaining where he was, Trace took another step in her direction. This time she forced herself to stand still. She crossed her arms across her midriff, fighting the natural instinct to get the hell away from him.

"I'll show myself around."

"Fine." She angled her chin in false bravado. "I'll just go for my run while you have a look-see. Be gone when I return." As she started past him, he snagged her wrist firmly enough to say he meant business.

"I've been assigned to protect you. You run, I run."

Her patience snapped. "Me Tarzan, you Jane."

"Yeah. Something like that."

She snatched her wrist away from him, pretending her heart wasn't thundering. She wouldn't need a cardio workout if he stayed under her roof another five minutes. His touch bothered her. His aggressive style bothered her. But what concerned her most was her own way too feminine reaction to him. "You're interrupting my schedule, Mr. Romero—Agent Romero. Whatever your name is."

"Trace."

She exhaled. He'd said it softly, a whisper of seduction. "You won't be here long enough for us to get that familiar."

"Don't count on it."

"Look, I appreciate what you're trying to do—"

"What I've been *ordered* to do."

"My sister overreacted, probably because *I* overreacted."

"Ms. Inamorata doesn't overreact." Patience wove through his tone. Maybe because he knew he would win. "If she thinks someone should protect your body and your secrets"—his glance started at her head and slowly traveled downward, igniting too-long-dormant senses—"then I'm going to be here for as long as she says."

"The police said they'd be happy to drive by."

"Periodically." He nodded. "But they're not going to provide the kind of protection I can."

"But—"

"Listen, Miss Inamorata. I'm here. And I don't need your permission to stay."

She tightened her ponytail. "Can I finish a sentence?"

"Depends whether you're going to agree with me or not." He grinned then, and strange things happened to her insides. "For the record," he continued, "there are other ways to shut you up. Who knows?" He leaned in a bit closer. "You might enjoy them. I would."

What the hell? No. Her heart increased its tempo to at least eighty-five percent of her target heart rate. She told herself he wouldn't kiss her, told herself she wouldn't let him if he tried.

The phone rang, mercifully shattering the moment.

"That'll be your sister, for me."

The phone trilled a second time.

She sighed. "Through there," she said, pointing toward the kitchen. It wasn't lost on her that he had won every battle thus far.

He nodded and headed into the heart of her home.

She trailed him, fully intending to eavesdrop.

"Bombs away!"

Scowling, Trace turned to look at her.

"Eureka!" she commanded. "No." *God, no.*

The incessant phone, the shrieking bird, her tension, all created sudden pandemonium. From everywhere at once, Eureka flew into the room, a fury of feathers and obnoxious squawks.

"Duck!" she warned.

Too late.

Eureka swooped low over Trace's head.

Aimee pushed her palms against her eyes, unable to watch.

"Crap!"

Her word exactly.

"Return to base," the parrot cried. "Return to base!"

The phone stopped ringing. Eureka landed on the perch on top of his cage. He rang a bell that hung beneath a mirror. "Mission accomplished!" Then silence, sudden and oppressive, echoed.

"Sorry about that," she said, slowly pulling her hands away from her face. "I should have warned you about his...tendencies."

"Does he do that a lot?"

"Only when he's upset. Hopefully he got the intruders. Bastards for leaving a door open, anyway. If anything happened to him—"

"I think he's okay," Trace said drily.

She was glad for his interruption. That ridiculous, bad-mannered bird was her best friend.

"Did he get me?" Trace ran a hand across the top of his head, then looked at his palm.

"You'll need to change your shirt," she said. For the first

time, she smiled at him. "Since you probably don't have another one, you can just go home."

"Stubborn woman."

"Stubborn man," she countered.

"It will wash." He dragged the hem from the waistband. "Err…"

He exposed part of his stomach, showing off his tight abs. *Damn.* Then he pulled the shirt a bit higher. "Don't!" she begged. "Please." Having him this close was bad enough. Half-naked would undo her.

The phone rang again. Looking at Trace, Eureka lifted a foot from the perch, as if considering his options.

"Eureka, no," she warned. He put his foot back down. "Good boy." But she, too, had her eye on Trace as he continued to the kitchen. His boots were loud on her hard-wood floor, and as large as he was, he dwarfed the space.

On the third ring, Trace picked up her phone. "Romero." He looked at her as he spoke to her sister. "No, ma'am. She hasn't been the least bit hospitable. I have a bruised foot and parrot shit on my shirt."

Rat bastard.

"Yeah, no problem." He held out the phone toward her.

Reluctantly she crossed to him, not wanting to get any closer to him than she needed to. Her mind might not have wanted him in her space, but her body most definitely did.

She took the device from him and, to her sister, said, "Hey."

He stood there, watching as her sister gave Aimee hell, finishing with, "We don't know what's going on. You have to think about yourself *and* the project."

"Exactly," Aimee agreed. Each day, the team drew closer to making the whole project work together. And the world would change when they succeeded. "Now you see the issue. I can't work with someone breathing down my neck."

"Is that what he's doing?"

Actually he *was* close enough that she could feel the warmth of him. And it wasn't all terrible. But it sure as hell was a distraction.

"I'm sure he'll do his best to stay out of your way."

"In a house this small? That's not possible."

"It's either Trace, or I will move you to a safe house. That's actually my preference."

"That would be traumatic for Eureka," Aimee protested.

"Those are your only choices, Aimee."

Aimee was the scientist, calm and rational, or she had been until ten minutes ago when Tall, Dark, and Dangerous showed up on her porch. She sighed.

"Do it for me?"

Trace's penetrating gaze was still on Aimee, heating her blood. "This is under duress."

"So noted."

She hung up.

"The formidable Ms. Inamorata wins another round?" His arms were folded across his chest, and he didn't gloat.

"Could you look smug or triumphant or something? It would be easier to dislike you that way."

"Surprisingly, some people like me."

She couldn't afford to be one of them, as easy as that promised to be with him standing only inches away and smelling so damn good. "You're right. That is surprising."

"When I first got here, I checked out the front of the house and the backyard. I wish you had a privacy fence rather than a chain-link one."

"The neighbors have a dog."

"Good to know. Now let's get the grand tour over with."

Did he ever give up? "You still need to wash your shirt."

"I have a duffel bag in my vehicle."

"Why am I not shocked?"

"Deductive reasoning? I understand you're a scientist."

"There is that." She couldn't help but smile. He was as charming as he was uncompromising.

"I fully intended to stay, regardless of your reception. I have workout clothes as well."

"But if we both go for a run, no one will be protecting the house."

"Wrong again. Your sister has assigned a couple of details. Bree Mallory and Daniel Riley are stationed in an SUV down the block. There's another team at the entrance to the subdivision."

"She thinks of everything."

He headed for the front door. "Be back in less than thirty seconds."

Aimee thought about locking him out, but the dark glance he shot her, combined with that set of his jaw, promised retribution if she crossed him. *His way.*

Standing in the doorway, she watched him jog across the road to his ridiculously large badass SUV. It resembled a military vehicle, capable of climbing anything or plowing through a lake. Faded denim hugged his powerful thighs and showed off his long legs. But if she were honest, she'd admit she liked the way they fit his taut ass. It appeared to be as nicely shaped and as honed as the rest of him.

Aimee mentally gave herself a shake. She shouldn't be having fantasies about her temporary jailer.

After grabbing an army-green duffel bag from the passenger seat, Trace slammed the door. He gave a thumbs-up signal to a white Suburban parked down the street—Mallory and Riley, he assumed—before jogging back to her.

Aimee took a step back to let him into the house.

"Should I change in your bedroom?"

"That's off-limits, I told you."

Right there, in the entryway, he pulled off the black cotton shirt.

She should have known better than to forbid him to do something.

Carefully he wadded the T-shirt. Even though she tried not to look, she was mesmerized. As she'd already surmised, he was seriously one sexy man. He had no excess fat around the middle, and a smattering of dark hair arrowed down the center of his chest to disappear behind the brass button holding his jeans together.

Her pulse easily reached eighty-seven, maybe eighty-eight, percent of her target heart rate. She didn't need her fitness monitor to tell her that. "I'll, uhm, throw that in the washer."

He handed her the T-shirt, then bent to unzip his bag.

"Is that a freaking gun tucked in your waistband?"

"Yeah," he said.

"No. No guns in my house. No way, no how."

He sighed, but he didn't stop riffling through his bag. And heaven help her, she couldn't help but cast a surreptitious glance at the contents, looking to see if he had underwear there. He pulled out a replacement black shirt, but she didn't see any boxers, briefs, or tighty whities. That realization revved her libido into overdrive.

"I mean it, Trace. No weapons."

He stood. "I appreciate that you don't want me here. I realize having a gun in your house is uncomfortable. I know I'll be invading your privacy."

"And?"

"Tough."

"Tough?"

He took her by the shoulders. "Tough."

Read more of *Trust In Me*.

ABOUT THE AUTHOR

I invite you to be the very first to know all the news by subscribing to my very special VIP Reader newsletter! You'll find exclusive excerpts, bonus reads, and insider information. https://www.sierracartwright.com/subscribe/

For tons of fun and to meet other awesome people like you, join my Facebook reader group: https://www.facebook.com/groups/SierrasSuperStars And for a current booklist, please visit my website www.sierracartwright.com

International bestselling author Sierra Cartwright was born in England, and she spent her early childhood traipsing through castles and dreaming of happily-ever afters. She was raised in Colorado and now calls Galveston, Texas home. She loves to connect with her readers, so please feel free to drop her a note.

[f] facebook.com/SierraCartwrightOfficial

[o] instagram.com/sierracartwrightauthor

[BB] bookbub.com/authors/sierra-cartwright

Donovan Dynasty

Bind

Brand

Boss

Mastered

With This Collar

On His Terms

Over The Line

In His Cuffs

For The Sub

In The Den

Made in United States
North Haven, CT
19 November 2021

11287135R00104